"Okay, what body part do you rely on most when you're riding a bull?"

Carly braced her hands on either side of her, just inches below her belt. "Right here. It's all in the hip action."

Smiling, Luke leaned forward, till their lips almost met. "Well, now," he breathed, "you are... absolutely...wrong."

"What?" She recoiled in astonishment and almost toppled off the fence.

He grabbed her around the waist to brace her, then took her hands and placed them on her thighs. He pressed his hands flat atop hers, his warm palms covering her fingers.

"Not the hips, Carly. A little lower. Here."

He rested his hands on her knees. Then he slid his palms upward again. A bolt of heat shot through her.

When he'd reached the midpoint of her thighs, he paused. "This is what'll keep you hanging on tight."

"Thanks for the tip." Her voice sounded too shaky.

Now she was sure he would make his move. Instead, he simply stepped back, leaving her to stand, stunned, on legs shakier than her voice.

Dear Reader,

One of my favorite story lines is a second chance at love, in which a hero and heroine—often with a troubled history together—split up but meet again years later. They long to triumph over whatever drove them apart, yet their conflict hasn't resolved itself. In fact, things have gotten worse.

That story line definitely fits Luke Nobel and Carly Baron. An argument and mutual pride once forced them to go their separate ways. Now Carly has come back home to find Luke managing her family's ranch. Instantly, their old attraction sparks to life. But Carly's hiding a secret she can never tell Luke....

I'm proud to have this book be part of a Harlequin American Romance continuity, in the lineup between such wonderful authors as Trish Milburn (*The Texan's Cowgirl Bride,* July 2014) and Pamela Britton (*The Texan's Twins,* September 2014). It has been a great pleasure to work with all the authors and editors involved in the series.

I hope you enjoy *The Texan's Little Secret.* I'd love to hear what you think about the story and to stay in touch. You can reach me at: P.O. Box 504 Gilbert, AZ 85299 or through my website: www.barbarawhitedaille.com. You can also find me on Facebook, www.facebook.com/barbarawhitedaille, and Twitter, twitter.com/barbarawdaille.

All my best to you.

Until we meet again,

Barbara White Daille

THE TEXAN'S LITTLE SECRET

BARBARA WHITE DAILLE

(H) HARLEQUIN® AMERICAN ROMANCE®

Special thanks and acknowledgment are given to Barbara White
Daille for her contribution to the Texas Rodeo Barons continuity.

Recycling programs
for this product may
not exist in your area.

ISBN-13: 978-0-373-75531-8

THE TEXAN'S LITTLE SECRET

Printed in U.S.A.

ABOUT THE AUTHOR

Barbara White Daille lives with her husband in the sunny Southwest, where they don't mind the lizards in their front yard but could do without the scorpions in the bathroom.

A writer from the age of nine and a novelist since eighth grade, Barbara is now an award-winning author with a number of novels to her credit.

When she was very young, Barbara learned from her mom about the storytelling magic in books—and she's been hooked ever since. She hopes you will enjoy reading her books and will find your own magic in them!

She'd also love to have you drop by and visit with her at her website, www.barbarawhitedaille.com.

Books by Barbara White Daille

HARLEQUIN AMERICAN ROMANCE

1131—THE SHERIFF'S SON
1140—COURT ME, COWBOY
1328—FAMILY MATTERS
1353—A RANCHER'S PRIDE
1391—THE RODEO MAN'S DAUGHTER
1416—HONORABLE RANCHER
1484—RANCHER AT RISK

To Kathleen Scheibling and Johanna Raisanen
Thank you for your support of my writing
and for always helping to bring out the best in my books.

And, as always and for everything, to Rich.

Chapter One

It didn't take Carly Baron long to figure out coming home to the Roughneck just might have been the worst decision she had ever made.

Every minute she stayed on the ranch, every second spent in her family's farm store, every moment anywhere near her dad pushed her closer to a confrontation with his ranch manager, the one man she never wanted to see again.

At the worktable in the back room of the Peach Pit, her thoughts shifted from the images she'd rather forget to the cartons she was filling with jars of preserves. She'd spent days out here at the store helping with new orders and most of this afternoon lending a hand to package them up. Finished with the final carton, she slapped the top of the box. "That ought to get these to their destination in good shape."

"I can't believe we're finally done," her older sister Savannah said. "I owe you, Carly. I've been so wrapped up in day-to-day business lately, I let the plans for expansion slide. That was a brilliant idea of yours for the targeted ad. This was my biggest order yet."

"No big deal." Carly shrugged. "Marketing 101. I need to get some use out of my degree. Selling Western wear wasn't exactly part of my five-year plan when I got out of college. And I'm glad you stuck to your guns about the store." The Peach Pit offered fresh produce and baked goods made from peaches and pecans grown on their farm, part of the Baron family's ranch.

Turning the small roadside stand into a full-fledged store had been Savannah's idea, one she had managed to implement and keep going despite resistance from their dad. Brock Baron never liked the thought of sinking capital into any endeavor he didn't control himself. His focus was—and always would be—on their North Texas ranch and on Baron Energies, the oil company he ran from the executive offices in a downtown Dallas high-rise.

"Daddy's got to see that this farm store's a little gold mine," she assured Savannah.

"Well, it's nowhere near there, yet. But it has the potential. Thanks to the ads, we've now got almost more orders than we can handle."

Carly put the tape dispenser back into its spot on the shelf and rested her hips against the worktable. "Speaking of orders, it's probably time for me to head back to the house to get mine."

Savannah shook her head. "And I'm sure Dad will have an entire list. You know we were all thrilled to have you come to visit a couple of months ago when Lizzie was in the hospital. But I'll confess we were overjoyed when you decided to come back again to stay for a while."

"I'll bet." Unwilling to think about her reasons for not returning to the ranch, Carly focused on what had finally brought her home—she was here to play nursemaid.

Seventy years old and as bullheaded as ever, Brock Baron also couldn't accept that the time had come for him to give up rodeoing and just let his kids continue to carry on the family tradition. His last seniors' event had left him with a broken leg and more aches and pains than he would ever admit to. Now, his enforced inaction was giving everyone else major headaches. "He was driving y'all nuts from the beginning, I'm sure."

"Oh, *that's* an understatement. Lucky for us, you've always been able to stand up to him."

"Another understatement." She'd be the first to acknowledge she had more than a little of their dad's hardheadedness in her.

They both laughed.

"Really, though," Savannah said. "How are you holding up?"

"Just fine. But I have to say, now that Daddy's reached the point he can get around by himself in that wheelchair, it's nerve-racking. I can never tell where and when he'll turn up in the house."

"Trust me, I know. It's only the fact he can't travel too far with it that's keeping me safe here at the store."

They smiled at each other.

Carly pushed away from the workbench, and Savannah reached out, surprising her with a hug. Her next-to-oldest sister had always been the quietest of the three girls in the Baron family.

"As much as I appreciate all your help this week," Savannah said, "I'm even happier just to have your company."

"Same here." To her surprise, she meant it. With a family of six kids, four of Brock's own and two stepsons, she had grown up lost in the middle of the crowd. Somehow, she had felt cut off from her sisters long before she'd left the Roughneck for college. With another young stepson of Brock's added to the mix shortly after that, the situation hadn't improved at all.

She still sometimes felt lost around the family but, on her past few visits, she had enjoyed spending more time with Savannah. "It's my pleasure to help you out here." She shook her head and laughed. "I need to do some manual labor. Sitting around the house is turning me soft. I can feel myself losing muscle tone."

"You're entitled to time off from babysitting Dad, you know. Don't you have any events coming up?"

Carly shook her head. "Not right away." They both barrel raced, though her sister made it out on the circuit less frequently than she did. "And I'm thinking of taking a break from racing, anyhow." Lately, it had become harder and harder for her to ramp up the enthusiasm for rodeo.

Or for anything else.

She forced a grin. "But enough about me. I imagine you're getting soft yourself. Although, maybe not." Tilting her head, she looked Savannah up and down. "After all, you're a newlywed. You ought to be getting plenty of another type of exercise to keep you in shape."

"Carly!" Savannah's cheeks flushed, but her eyes sparkled.

"Hey, don't play innocent with me. You know my so-called crazy advice helped you get what you wanted."

Otherwise known as a brand-new husband.

Savannah and their older sister, Lizzie, had both found their true loves recently. Carly swallowed a sigh. A forever relationship wasn't in the cards for her. Not now, maybe not ever, and she'd just have to live with that. Still, she wished her sisters—wished the four of them, counting their new significant others—all the best in the world.

"Will I see you over at the house at supper?" she asked.

Savannah shook her head. "No, I've got a stew going in the slow cooker."

"Smart move, moving into the apartment upstairs when Daddy expanded the building."

"Believe me, now that he's home full-time, I'm thanking my lucky stars I made the decision."

"Come on, he's not so bad." *Neither am I, even if we are like two peas in a pod.* And why did she feel the sudden desire to state her case to Savannah? Getting more comfortable around her was one thing. Getting close enough to spill sisterly secrets wasn't gonna happen. "Talk to you later," she said, heading toward the main room of the farm store.

"Carly?"

She turned back.

"I forgive you for your smart remark about exercise, but...speaking of Travis—"

"Were we speaking of Travis? I didn't hear anyone mention the name."

"Stop." Smiling, Savannah swatted her arm. Then her expression turned serious. "You haven't asked about his progress."

"No," she said, just as seriously, her heart missing a beat.

Twenty years earlier, their mother had left the ranch, abandoning them all. Just this spring, Savannah had hired Travis, an old school friend and now her husband, who worked as a private detective, to track down Delia Baron. Not an easy job, as it turned out. They'd now reached the beginning of July with still no substantial developments. Or...

"Did he have luck with that connection to Albuquerque?" She hid her clenched fists at her sides and stared, waiting.

"No, it turned out to be another dead end." Savannah sighed. "I know you're trying not to breathe down my neck about Travis's search, the way I'm trying not to hover over his shoulder."

But Carly would *like* to hover over his shoulder. Heck, she wanted to help with the search and hurry things up any way she could.

Yes, when it came to comparing her to their dad, the apple—or maybe the peach—didn't fall far from the tree. "Well, don't give up," she said, attempting to sound reassuring. "I'm sure if he just keeps digging, Travis will catch a break soon."

Outside, sunlight dazzled her eyes before she could slip on her sunglasses, and heat seemed to haze the peach-scented air. Even with the high temperature, the short ride to the main house didn't warrant turning on the ranch truck's air conditioner. It would barely cool the interior before she arrived.

She left the windows open and drove slowly, appreciating the time alone. The time to breathe.

That last thought reminded her of her sister's comments about breathing and hovering.

Savannah had assumed she'd hung back from asking questions about the search to keep from pressuring Travis. Partly true. But, for the most part, she walked around nearly biting her tongue in half to keep the two of them from guessing how eagerly she wanted results. She had her own need to find their mom and, like her reasons for staying away from the ranch, it was one her sisters and brothers didn't know. If she had her way, they would *never* know.

A FEW MINUTES LATER, Carly nosed the truck into the long drive to the ranch house. The open windows caught a cross breeze, mild but welcome.

Several yards from the house, she glanced toward the barn and saw a sight she didn't welcome at all.

Everything about her tightened—her hands on the wheel, her shoulders, her throat, her breath.

The cowboy standing in the barn doorway started toward the truck, his long legs in worn jeans eating up the space rapidly. He wore a battered Stetson, the wide brim shading most of his face, but no matter how much she tried to convince herself this was just any old cowhand striding toward her, she couldn't believe the lie.

There was no mistaking those mile-wide shoulders or that sandy-blond hair. No mistaking the way her heart pounded.

The last time she'd seen Luke Nobel, he had turned and stalked away from her in anger, leaving her teenage heart crushed in the dust beneath his boots. To this day, she hadn't healed right and probably never would.

She wasn't ready for this meeting.

He wasn't giving her a choice.

Seconds later, he halted within arm's reach of her driver's door, his eyes seeming to hold the power to pin her into her seat.

All these weeks of worrying, and here was the one situation she had wanted to avoid. All the years of running, and here stood the one man she'd tried so hard to leave behind.

"Carly Baron," he said. "At last."

His voice rumbled deeper than it had years before, coming from a chest broader and more solid than the boy's she remembered.

"Luke." She forced a grin. "Isn't this flattering. Sounds like you were just waiting for the chance to run into me."

"I figured it was bound to happen, once Brock said you'd come home again. But when I never caught sight of you, I started to wonder if he'd been hitting the pain pills too hard."

"No pills. And, to Daddy's dismay, we take great care in measuring out the bourbon. Also, I'm not home again. I'm just visiting."

"The helpful daughter."

"That's me all over." Her body tingled when he continued to stare. Gripping the steering wheel, she fought back a wave of disgust at herself. If she let a mere look from this man bring that reaction on, she would soon find herself in a world of hurt from him. Again.

She had parked at the wrong angle to allow for a quick exit to the house, and the truck sat too far from the road to reverse all the way down the drive. Maybe she could just back up a bit and then run over his danged toes.

The thought brought on a smile.

"Excuse me." She shoved open the door and he jumped back.

A double dose of attitude made her stand straight in front of him. He stared back without saying a word. Let him look all he wanted. One touch, though, and she'd deck him.

The silence stretched on, till her nerves began to feel stretched thin, too. *Never let 'em see you sweat,* an old rodeo clown had once told her. She'd go that one better. *Never let Luke see you care.* She waved her hand in front of him. "Hel-loo. I'm still here. No sense trying to act like I've disappeared in a puff of smoke."

"Not yet, anyhow. I was just thinking. It's been a long time."

"And you've come a long way." If he picked up on the added meaning behind her words, he didn't show it. Anger at his reminder of their past couldn't quite overcome the hurt. Still, she managed to keep her voice even. "I hear you're manager now. Daddy's right-hand man. You finally made the connection and landed a job on the Roughneck, the way you'd always wanted."

He got that message, all right. His jaw hardened, and his chest rose with a deep breath, as if he'd had to summon his patience.

What did he expect—that she would have forgotten the way he'd tried to use her to get a job on her dad's ranch?

"Maybe I had other reasons for showing up that day, besides the job."

"What reasons? Trying to win me over?" She laughed without humor. "Why bother, when you already had me where you wanted me?"

"You think that's what it was all about? I wanted to get to your daddy through you?"

"I said that to you then, and you didn't argue. But it looks like you found a way without me, after all."

He stared at her for a long moment before shaking his head. "Funny. By now, I would have thought you'd grown up some."

The pity in his tone rubbed her nerves raw. "I expected you'd have grown beyond working for my daddy."

"A man's gotta have a job," he said mildly. "And I guess none of us knows what the future has in store."

"I'm not concerned about the future, only in what's

happening today. *And* in making sure not to repeat the past."

"Yeah. Well, what's happening in my world today includes managing this ranch. I'd better get back to it."

"That's what Daddy pays you for," she said, forcing a lightness that vied with the heaviness in her heart.

He touched the brim of his Stetson. "See you around." *Not if I can help it.*

He turned and walked away with enough of a tight-jeaned swagger to make her breath catch.

She leaned back against the sun-warmed truck, bombarded by memories she'd tried for so long to forget. Memories of that innocent, insecure high-school girl who always blended into the woodwork. Who had felt lost in the crowd of her own family. And who could never push away the vision of herself as a little girl her own mother couldn't love.

At least, not enough to make her stay.

Not even being the apple of her daddy's eye could make up for all that.

Just once, she'd wanted someone to single her out, to notice her differences, to see her as an individual, not as simply one of the Baron brood.

She had thought she'd found that someone in Luke Nobel.

She couldn't have been more wrong. Or been so betrayed.

Pushing herself away from the truck, she crossed her arms over her chest and glared at him as he made his retreat. Their first meeting in seven years had gone no better than she'd expected, no worse than she'd feared.

Regardless of what he thought, she had grown up since the days they were together. Toughened up, too.

And yet she wished this could be the last time she would ever see him.

All the needs and secrets and sorrows she kept from her family had to be kept from Luke, as well.

Especially from Luke.

He was a big part of the reason she had so much to hide.

Chapter Two

In the foyer of the main house, Carly paused to take inventory. Her breathing had returned to its usual even rhythm. The flush of anger warming her cheeks could be attributed to the heat outside. Only her hands might give her away. They continued to shake in irritation over the meeting with Luke. Whether or not the tremble would be visible to anyone else's eye, she didn't know. But she wasn't about to get caught out here, checking her reactions in the hall mirror.

After plastering a smile on her face, she crossed to the living room. Brock sat in the wheelchair with his leg extended, a file folder in his hands and papers spread across the cushions of the couch beside him.

Before she could say a word, he grumbled, "This is no way to conduct business. I ought to bring the damned desk from the den in here."

"The boys told you they'd happily move it for you." Her brothers would do anything to help cut down on Brock's crankiness. Deliberately, she had just now done the opposite, giving him a chance to be contrary. Letting off some steam with her might make him ease up on the rest of the family.

Sure enough, he snapped, "Moving furniture still wouldn't get things done properly."

"And you probably wouldn't be happy, anyway, unless you could spread everything across that ginormous conference table you've got downtown. But that's out for now. If you've been listening to your doctor, you know that won't happen for a while yet." Lord only knew much longer she'd be needed here. How much longer she could force herself to stick around.

She picked up the edge of the afghan trailing on the floor and fluffed the pillow behind his back.

"Stop messing. This isn't a sick room."

"Yessir." Biting her lip to hold back a smile, she studied him. Tall and slim, he had a vigorous head of hair, pure silver now. His eyes, bright blue against his slightly weatherworn skin, didn't miss much. They never had.

She moved to perch on the arm of the couch. The paperwork spread below her might have started out in neat piles but now lay haphazardly across the cushions, threatening to slip to the floor. "Anything I can help you with?"

"Not unless you've learned how to take dictation."

"Why, Daddy—" she batted her lashes "—I'm an expert at it. Thanks to you, I'm now dictated to on a daily basis."

"Don't be fresh."

She laughed, knowing she was the only one of his kids who could get away with smart-mouthing him.

Or, *usually* get away with it.

Leaning forward, she kissed his temple. "You should be more grateful to have me here. Admit it. Sparring with me gives you another reason to get up in the morning."

He grunted and turned a page in the file, but she saw the tic in his cheek and knew he had fought back a smile.

"Come on, let's get some of your paperwork taken care of. My handwriting has to be better than your chicken scratches." With a notepad and pencil from the desk held ready, she prepared to take notes. "Go slowly, and I'll write in longhand."

They went through one batch of paper after another. Carly jotted memos to be typed up by his secretary and directions to be passed along to various members of his staff, including her oldest sister, Lizzie, who had temporarily taken over as acting president of Baron Energies.

With the flood of papers finally corralled and roped into neat piles, Brock sat back and eyed her as if seeing her for the first time that day. "What are you doing around here, anyhow? Aren't you planning to do some traveling soon?"

"Home to Houston, you mean?" she said, deliberately misunderstanding. "Are you already tired of me hanging around?"

"That's ridiculous. I'm talking about competing. You're keeping up with your skills, aren't you?"

"Of course. But you know what they say about all work and no play. I'm not competing this weekend."

"Why not?"

"I didn't want to sign up anywhere. Not for barrel racing, anyhow. I'm ready to give it up."

"Don't be absurd. You've barely gotten your saddle broken in."

"You can hardly say that when I've been competing since the age of four."

"Yes, and you haven't done badly," he said grudgingly. "You've got what it takes to go all the way to the top, if you'll just settle down and focus. But you won't get far competing only part-time." His eyes narrowed. "And backing off isn't going to help. You need to put everything into it if you want to be the best."

She shrugged. "Maybe I don't care about being the best. Maybe I'm bored."

"Bored, hell. You can't walk away from this—rodeo's in your blood. In your genes."

"I know. I didn't say I'd give up rodeo, just barrel racing. My heart's not in it anymore." She made a mental bet on how long it would take him to go ballistic once he heard her next statement—probably about half a second. But it would be guaranteed to get him off her back about not competing lately. "I'm going to try bull riding."

He barely allowed her to finish her sentence. "And do what?" he demanded, gesturing at his elevated leg. "Crack yourself up, like I did? Don't be foolish. You leave that event to the boys and stick to your barrels." Raising his chin, he glared at her.

She lowered her chin, so like his, and stared back.

Only the sudden rapid click of high heels on the foyer floor made her break eye contact with him.

Brock's wife, Julieta, entered the living room. "Hello, you two. How's the patient?"

Brock made a derisive sound.

She smiled. "Carly, I'll take over now, if you have things you want to do before supper." She slid the plum-colored suit jacket from her shoulders. "I'll go up and change as soon as I run a few items of business past your father."

Carly nodded. Julieta must have picked up on the tension in the room. She gave the woman credit for providing her with a graceful escape.

She gave Julieta credit for a lot of things. As well as being Brock's third wife, she managed the public relations department at Baron Energies. She was good at her job, good at handling folks—and her husband. Knowing his wife went into the office every morning while he sat confined to the ranch had to help keep Brock's crankiness level…well…cranked up. But it didn't keep Julieta from taking care of business.

"See you in a bit." Carly smiled at Brock in farewell. He nodded.

As she took the stairs to her room, she held back a laugh. Who knew how long that stalemate between them would have lasted if Julieta hadn't walked in.

She didn't care. No matter what, she wouldn't have backed down on the statement she'd made about bull riding.

Once, she had thought she would never get enough of barrel racing, of the thrill of commanding her mount, honing her skill, increasing her speed. But since she'd left the ranch, with each year that had gone by, her interest and enthusiasm had waned by ever-increasing degrees. Though her eyes stayed on the prize, the motivating spark was gone.

And she needed a spark. A lure. A challenge. She needed *something* to make her feel whole again.

Like Brock, she needed a reason to get up in the morning.

"IF THIS DAMNED contraption doesn't turn out to be the death of me, that girl will," Brock Baron said, slapping his hand on the arm of the wheelchair.

His wife placed her briefcase next to the piles of paperwork on the couch. "And why is that?"

"She's a worry to me in general. Always has been. You're well aware of the reasons, including the fact she hasn't spent more than a handful of weeks on this ranch since she finished high school."

"A slight exaggeration."

He shrugged. "Fair enough. But there's no denying she's the least settled of any of the kids."

"She is settled, Brock. Just out of the area."

And out of his range of influence. That didn't sit well with him at all. Not for any of his offspring, and especially not for Carly.

Now that his being laid up had caused her to spend some time at the Roughneck again, he'd had the chance to confirm his fears. "She's as wild as she ever was, and I don't see her wanting to change."

"In view of all the time you two have spent together, coming home probably hasn't helped that."

"Meaning what?"

"As you always tell me, she's the child who most takes after you in temperament."

He couldn't deny that. To borrow a phrase, she was a chip off the old Baron block. But he'd never tell his wife—or anyone—that Carly's ways made him hold a soft spot in his heart for her. "What are you saying?"

"I'd guess neither one of you realizes, but spending so much time together has only reinforced how alike you are."

"And you're insinuating that's a bad thing?"

She laughed. "No, of course not. But considering she's young and female, she doesn't need to come across quite so strong on some of your traits."

"She needs her head set on straight, that's what she needs," he grumbled. "Bad enough she won't live on the ranch or work at the family business. And now there's this damned-fool idea she's come up with."

"Ah. I thought I saw daggers drawn when I came in here. What is it?"

"She's got it into her mind she wants to give up barrel racing."

Her eyebrows rose. "You mean quit the rodeo? Now, that does surprise me."

"No, not quit." He could barely bring himself to share what his youngest daughter had said. "She tells me she wants to go in for bull riding."

Julieta looked at him thoughtfully. "Why does that bother you? It's all part of the tradition, isn't it?"

"Not for the women of this family."

"Maybe not originally. But times change. And it's more common now for women to ride bulls."

"It's damned dangerous, that's what it is." He exhaled heavily. "At any rate, what's the point of my having it out with the girl? As headstrong as she is, she's sure to want to ride despite my arguments."

"Or because of them."

"That, too." Again, he slapped the arm of the wheelchair. "And I'm going to have to do something about it."

"YOU THINK LUKE will show up before the barbecue's over?" Kim Healy leaned against the counter in the ranch house kitchen. Her brown eyes, opened wide, counteracted her offhand tone.

Carly shrugged. They had returned to the house for reinforcements, including another batch of the homemade biscuits that Anna, their cook and housekeeper since long before Carly had been born, had left in the still-warm oven. She looked at Kim and pointed toward the stove. "I haven't got the first clue about Luke Nobel's plans."

"You would have, if you'd been back here the past couple of years."

Carly gnawed her lower lip. Kim wouldn't let this ride.

Every Fourth of July, Brock laid on a barbecue for his family and any of the hands who were around to attend.

Once she'd heard Luke had started working on the ranch, she had deliberately begun missing the event, using her job in Houston as an excuse, even though it meant passing up Anna's barbecued beef.

Fortunately, Anna knew her well. The casual meal always showed up on the menu during her infrequent visits.

"In all this time taking care of your dad, you must have seen Luke by now," Kim persisted. "Have you talked to him yet?"

"Briefly." Two days ago, and she still felt unsettled by the memory. Not that she'd need to confess that to Kim, who would already know. And she couldn't blame Kim for her question.

They had been fast friends since second grade, when Kim had tried to take over in a kickball game. Carly had punched her lights out and, to her delight, Kim had punched back. Someone squealed about the tussle to their teacher, which resulted in Mrs. Blake's frog-marching them to the principal. She and Kim had sat waiting in the hallway outside his office, both of them covered in dust from the unpaved playground, sporting a rapidly swelling eye and a bloodied nose, respectively, and grinning at each other.

"Briefly," Kim repeated in a low tone, though they were alone in the room. "That one word is speaking volumes to me. And what did you speak to *him* about? What did he say to you?"

"Not much." Sad, really, when she and Luke once had so much to talk about.

"He's still single, Carly, and since there's never any gossip floating around about his love life, that means he doesn't have one. Which means he's unattached. He works for your dad, he takes care of his daughter—you know Rosie's two already, right? He helps out his mom. Once in a while he stops at the Longhorn for a couple of beers. And that's about it."

"Enough already, Kim."

"Don't you even care that he's still up for grabs?"

"What I care about are those biscuits." Carly gestured toward the oven again. "We've got a herd of hungry cowboys waiting out there." After taking a sleeve of plastic cups from the pantry, she urged Kim toward the back door.

She couldn't blame her best friend for her curiosity. Since that day in the schoolyard, Kim had been the one whose shoulder she'd cried on at Christmas and on her birthday, the days she had most missed the mom who'd gone away and left them all. Kim had been the friend she had ranted to a few years after her mom's departure, when Brock had remarried. Adding her first stepmother and two stepbrothers into her life, making the family even larger, had thrown Carly into the middle of the crowd that had left her feeling so lost.

Kim was still the one she told all her secrets to.

Or almost all of them.

Outside, the ranch hands milled around the yard, already lining up for seconds at the serving table Carly and Kim had loaded down with Anna's ovenproof dishes of ribs, baked beans and potatoes in their jackets.

At another table, her sisters presided over an assembly line of pop bottles. A few feet away, her brother, Jet, had set up the beer keg.

Kim veered toward one of the tables spread with food.

Carly walked up to Jet. "Hey, little brother." She never missed a chance to greet him with the teasing reminder he was a year younger. "Don't drink too much of that poison. We've got a date for tomorrow, remember? And when I take you on at the arena, I don't want you claiming a handicap because you're hungover."

"Are you kidding? This stuff doesn't bother me. I'll tell you what does rile me," he added loudly enough to make sure Savannah and Lizzie heard him. "Getting stuck with the tough job today."

"What's so hard about filling up a beer mug?" Carly asked.

"Filling it isn't the problem. It's having to hand it off to somebody else."

She laughed. "Don't even try for a sympathy vote from me. You've never in your life had to give up something you didn't want to. I'm sure you'll get your fill."

"Don't waste time worrying over it," Savannah called to her.

"That's for sure," Lizzie said. "He's already had more than his share."

"Somebody had to taste test," Jet protested. "Savannah didn't want any, and in your delicate condition, Lizzie, you need to stay away from it."

For just a moment, Carly let herself glance at her sister's rounded stomach, where the first Baron baby of the next generation waited to make an appearance. When Lizzie caught her eye, she forced a smile. She had so much she wanted to say to Lizzie, so many questions she could never ask.

Do you worry about carrying the baby to term? Did you miss not sharing the news with Mom? Do you hate knowing you can't turn to her for advice?

After Lizzie's health scare early on in the pregnancy, Carly had kept those concerns and questions, those reminders of the past, all to herself. Yet they were concerns she had always wondered about, too.

Attempting to swallow the lump in her throat, she

forced a smile. She moved past Lizzie's table and continued to the one filled with plates and plastic utensils set up assembly-line style. Kim now stood talking to one of the cowhands. Carly couldn't help but glance around the yard, looking for a familiar broad-shouldered cowboy. There were plenty of cute wranglers in the vicinity, but not the one she...wanted to avoid.

Darn Kim, anyway, for bringing up Luke's name.

As if he hadn't already been on her mind.

A moment later, Kim hurried up to her. "Well, don't look now, but you're about to get your chance to make up for that brief encounter." Her voice practically vibrated with excitement. "You-know-who's headed this way."

"Knock it off, Kim. We're not kids anymore. Grown women don't get all excited just because there's a man around."

"Then why are you turning as red as you used to in high school?"

"Anger. Irritation. Pique." She grinned. "Now, *there's* a vocabulary word. You make sure and tell Mrs. Blumfeld I didn't forget her ninth-grade English classes." Kim's glance past her told the truth of the matter about Luke. "He's only headed this way for more of Anna's barbecued beef, and the table's almost right behind us."

"Oh, no, he's way past that point."

Luke couldn't want to talk to her. And she certainly didn't want to chat with him. Then why did her pulse jump at the thought? Maybe because no one in the family had ever seen them together. As far as the Barons knew... well, as far as she *knew* they knew...she and Luke had never met each other.

And it would be best to keep it that way.

Kim carried her plate and utensils over to the next table.

"I'll take one of those." The deep voice gave her the clue. She didn't need to see the cowboy's face to know Luke had come up to stand beside her. He reached for a cup.

Her fingers tightened automatically, crinkling the wrapping.

He eyed the package. "I can skip having something to drink if you're that attached to the cups."

"I'm not attached to them. I'm wondering what you're doing here." *Darn*. The truth wasn't at all what she'd meant to say.

His eyebrows shot up. "It's a barbecue. I'll give you three guesses."

One of the cowboys edged by them to get to the picnic table.

Luke stepped aside, moving closer to her. Her hands clenched. The plastic wrapper from the cups crackled again. She thought about walking away. That ought to show him how little their conversation meant to her. But he stood blocking the pathway between the tables. She couldn't pass without brushing against him. The immediate shiver of anticipation running up her spine showed just how foolish *that* move would be.

There was nothing behind her to give her an excuse to go in that direction. Besides, no way would she would let him—or anyone—see her run. Instead, she stood her ground, trying to ignore how awkward she felt. Trying to forget she'd experienced that same feeling the first time she'd met him. "Never mind the three guesses. I just meant you surprised me. I didn't see you around."

"Keeping an eye out for me?"

"Not hardly." What was he doing, anyhow? Flirting with her? "Let me tell you, if you're trying to act cute, you're missing it by a country mile. And if you're hoping to keep up appearances in front of the boss, don't bother. He's not looking our way."

The cowboy who had passed them had gotten what he wanted from the table and moved on. She needed to do the same with Luke. "Oh, and if you have any idea about trying to repeat history, forget it. This time, *I'm* walking away. Enjoy your barbecue."

She slipped by him, bumping her hip on the edge of the picnic table. As she had expected, in the tight space, she couldn't avoid brushing against his arm. The warmth of his skin left hers tingling. For a moment she froze, then she pushed past him, leaving him in the dust.

She hurried to catch up to Kim.

They filled their plates and found an empty picnic bench off to one side of the yard. To her irritation, she discovered Luke hard on her heels.

Chapter Three

Kim set her plate down but didn't take a seat. "I forgot napkins. Be right back."

"Get some extra," Carly called after her. She gritted her teeth and scooted onto one of the benches. Luke settled opposite as if she'd invited him to join her. "What's this? I told you, you don't need to make nice with the boss's daughter."

"I learned that lesson already," he said in a low tone. "I was nice to you once. You threw that in my face."

Was he trying to imply she had been the one at fault years ago? "Then I can't image why you want to sit here. Couldn't you find a seat anywhere else?"

"Could have. But I'm too polite to walk off in the middle of a conversation." He paused, as if waiting for her to pounce on the statement. But she'd already made her point about his walking away from her. When she said nothing, he went on, "To tell you the truth, it's a surprise to me, too, seeing you here, considering you don't make a habit of attending the barbecue."

"I try never to do the expected."

He nodded. "Some things never change. I guess you wouldn't be here now, either, if not for coming home to take care of your daddy."

He sat looking at her. She stared back into those eyes

that had once fascinated her. Such a unique shade of golden brown. The same amber hue as a jar of dark honey, so warm and sweet and—

Darn. She lowered her hands beneath the edge of the table and curled her fingers into fists. She had handled seeing Luke again. She could sit here pretending to have a polite conversation in front of her family. But she sure didn't need long-forgotten memories sneaking up on her, hitting her when she was least prepared for them.

"Since we're on the subject of surprises," he added, "I have to say it was strange I never ran into you at any of the rodeos."

"So sorry to disappoint you. Did you think I'd follow your career so I could hound your heels, like the rest of your buckle bunnies?"

He grinned. "You must've followed something, if you knew about them."

"How could I not know?" she asked, keeping her tone as honey-sweet as his eyes. "Even the wannabe champs on the circuit have their admirers."

And Luke had been so much more than a wannabe. A bull-riding champion, one of the youngest on record, with one of the *best* records in rodeo. "I kept track of you, all right. For exactly the opposite reason—to know when and where you'd be competing so I could head off in the opposite direction."

"Then it must've made things easier for you when I quit rodeoing."

"I couldn't have cared less." *Liar.* His decision might have sent a shockwave through the rodeo community, but it had sure made her life less...stressed. Until she'd found out he had taken a job at the Roughneck. "But I'll bet it made my daddy happy to know he could have you working for him."

To her annoyance, he grinned. "I reckon it did. I'll tell you what's making him happy right now. Having you around again. The rest of the family likes it, too."

And you, Luke? Her throat tightened as she held back the question. She had no desire to think about anything happening between them. She had already spent too much time thinking about what might have been, about what she once could have had but had lost.

Her throat tightening even more at the thought, she looked over her shoulder. Her so-called best friend stood near the drinks table, hanging out with Lizzie and Savannah. Great. Kim was keeping her distance. Giving her time alone with Luke. Just what she didn't want.

Reluctantly, almost feeling his gaze on her, she turned back. "I told you the other day, I'm only here temporarily. Just while my family needs me."

He nodded. "Guess you're eager to get back home. I hear you're still living down in Houston."

Was he keeping tabs on her? She swallowed her irritation and fought to keep her tone polite. There were too many people around for her to respond the way she really wanted to. "After college, I wanted to stay on. I like it there." *Double liar.*

"What's the attraction that's got you keeping yourself way down there?"

"It's only a couple of hours away. I've got a job. I'm in sales for a company that manufactures Western wear. It's small, family-owned, like the Peach Pit."

"You couldn't get me to live in the big city. Besides, you don't miss your folks?"

"Of course I do."

"You don't visit often."

"That doesn't mean I don't love my family. When Lizzie had…a health scare a few months back, I was here on the double. But I'm happy to have a life of my own, away from the ranch."

How many more lies could she tell in one conversation? She wasn't happy in Houston. Far from it. But she had fought for the choice to go to school there...just as she had fought to stay. It was easier than coming home and facing everything. Her childhood. Her history. Luke.

He would never know any of that. She would tell him one truth, though. "It's a nice feeling, knowing I can take care of myself."

He paused with the last bite of barbecued beef sandwich halfway to his mouth, then nodded. "I can understand that. I want my daughter to feel the same way—once she grows up, that is."

Another topic she had no desire to deal with. "I'm happy to be independent."

His eyebrows rose. "Is that what you call cutting yourself off from family?"

"What do you know about my relationship with my family? It's been a long time since the days I used to share my troubles with you." All too aware of the crowd around them, she forced a smile. "And I didn't cut myself off. I learned how to live on my own. That's something no one can take away from me."

"Don't be so sure," he said softly.

Though he smiled, too, her heart skipped a beat at his suddenly bleak expression.

Unable to meet his eyes, she pushed a stray olive around on her plate with a fork and inhaled an uneven breath. She couldn't handle seeing that unexpected touch of vulnerability in Luke's face. She didn't want to dwell on what had happened in his life once he'd walked away from her. Most of all, she couldn't bear even to think about his grief over the wife he had lost or his love for the little girl he shared with that other woman.

To her relief, Kim finally returned to the table, bringing the napkins she'd supposedly needed. To her even greater relief, Luke grabbed his plate and cup.

"Take my seat," he said. "I've got to be getting home."

He nodded at them both.

Watching him walk away set off a familiar ache in the pit of her stomach.

Kim slid into the seat Luke had left. Carly welcomed the distraction, though Kim's eyes already held questions. She would want to know what she'd missed. Carly couldn't fault her for that. When it came to Luke, Kim had been in on the ground floor of Carly's grand plan.

In senior year, she and Kim had both considered it a real coup for her to have snagged an "older" man, just on the verge of twenty-one compared to their eighteen. Obviously, despite knowing how hurt she had been over the breakup, her best friend believed she still had a thing for Luke.

"And, so…?" Kim prompted.

Carly shrugged. Under cover of the talk all around them, she lowered her voice and reported, "He sat. He ate. He departed. That was the extent of our big reunion, and that's all it's ever going to be."

"Come on, Carly, you can't be immune to the guy. He's twice as hot as he was when you went with him."

"And any interest I had in Luke Nobel cooled to sub-zero temperatures back then. It's not like he meant a lot to me, anyhow," she fibbed. "You know I only went out with him in the first place to try to get my dad off my back." That had been her intention anyhow.

Too bad she had sabotaged herself.

No matter how strongly she'd objected, with graduation on the horizon, Brock had grown more adamant than ever about her taking her place at Baron Energies. At a desk job.

She had acted out, doing the worst thing she could think of—the only thing she could think of at the time— to make Brock Baron change his mind. She had dated Luke Nobel. Being an "older man" and living in a poor part of town earned an automatic two strikes against him—at least on her daddy's list of high standards.

Yes, the perfect plan...

"But then you never told your dad anything about Luke," Kim said. "You never told your family or anybody but me. Why not?"

Carly shrugged. For some strange reason, after her first date with Luke, her feelings about flaunting him in front of Brock and her family had done a one-eighty. "I didn't need him for leverage anymore. I decided to get a backbone and stand up for myself, instead. I told Daddy point-blank I just had no interest in a job at Baron Energies. Then I flashed my acceptance letter from Houston at him and informed him I would be leaving town."

Kim gasped. "You never told me that, either. How did he react?"

"As if I'd tossed a cow pie down in front of him."

"You probably broke his heart. You should've listened to me about drinking and drugs. *Those* would've had your dad changing his mind altogether about wanting you on the payroll."

And just look who he had on his payroll now.

Carly choked on a laugh. "As if you really meant the suggestions seriously."

"You know I didn't." Kim sighed. "Well, I'm sorry it didn't turn into the romance of the century. But even if you never told anyone, after all, I guess going out with Luke was better than my alternatives."

If she only knew.

But how could she tell Kim the truth? She couldn't explain, even to her own satisfaction, why she had suddenly felt the need to keep Luke all to herself. Instead, she had sworn Kim to silence.

Still, typical teen that she was back then, she couldn't keep from sharing developments with her best friend.

Day by day, she had filled in every little detail of her first big romance…until the part where she and Luke slept together.

THREE LONG, LONG DAYS after the barbecue, Luke sat at the bar of the Longhorn, the local saloon. He took a deep, satisfying swallow of beer from the mug in front of him.

His mom had gone to her usual Monday-night get-together with her cronies, bringing Rosie along. The ladies all claimed to take their card games seriously, but he suspected the women paid more attention to dessert and his daughter than they did to their poker hands.

He thought about the endless weekend, starting with Friday and the barbecue he never should have gone to. Not when he knew Carly Baron was back on the Roughneck and would be there, too.

On Saturday, he'd kept busy with his men, handling the backbreaking job of clearing brush. The hard labor kept his body moving, and working with a couple of cowhands who always had their mouths in gear kept him from thinking thoughts he shouldn't. He'd chosen to work side-by-side with those men for that very reason.

On Sunday…well, that was a mite tougher. If the Longhorn had been open, he might've stopped in for a brew and some company to distract him. Instead, he'd spent the slow summer afternoon with his mom and Rosie, his two-year-old daughter, who were his first choice of company, anyhow.

At least, Rosie was, always. His mom, not so much. Not when he had something on his mind. When he had worries, he also had all he could do to keep them from her sharp eyes. Somehow, yesterday, he had managed to get by without getting the third degree about anything.

And today, he'd cleared his mind of Carly again.

He intended to keep it cleared.

He breathed a sigh of relief at his own determination, took a last slug of his beer and set the empty mug back on the bar.

"Fill you up again?" the bartender asked.

Luke nodded, then watched the man walk away with the mug.

"Good service," commented the guy a couple of stools to his right. He wore dress pants and too-shiny shoes. "Hope it stays that quick."

"It won't once the crowd gets here," Luke told him. Between the locals, whose Monday-morning quarterbacking usually lasted through the evening, and the city slickers like the one next to him, who liked to live life rough in the 'burbs, the bar wouldn't be quiet for long.

He glanced into the wall-length mirror lined with liquor bottles. It reflected most of the room as well as the Longhorn's double glass doors, which had just opened to admit a couple of females. Familiar females. The one he took note of was hot and blonde and loaded for bear, judging by her expression when she caught his reflection in the glass.

So much for clearing his mind of Carly Baron.

"You sound like a regular," the guy next to him said.

"I stop in once in a while." For two or three beers,

his limit. He'd come tonight more to get away from his empty house and his own thoughts than to have a brew. And now look where that idea had gotten him.

Carly wore jeans that hugged her hips and a shirt of some shimmery fabric. With every little move she made, the shirt caught the glow from the neon advertisements hung around the barroom. He tried not to follow the flashes of light in the mirror as she and her friend Kim sauntered across the sawdust-covered floor to seats at the far end of the bar.

The guy to his right gave a low whistle. "Now, *there's* a real babe."

Luke clamped his jaw shut.

Once, Carly had meant everything to him. But that was years ago, before she'd accused him of using her to get ahead. Before she'd joined the ranks of folks who didn't believe he could succeed on his own.

Yeah, at the barbecue, Carly had hit the mark with her crack about making nice with the boss's daughter. He *had* gone out of his way to talk with her, the way he stayed friendly with all Brock Baron's kids.

But, more to the point, the truth was, he'd chatted her up to show himself he could do it and walk away again. To prove she didn't mean anything to him anymore. And he'd done exactly that, hadn't he? She was just another woman to him now, right?

A few people occupied stools between him and the women, but he could still see her in the mirror, her blond hair spilling over her shoulders and down her back, almost reaching the waistband of those snug jeans of hers. All too aware of his own jeans suddenly hugging tight, he shifted on his stool.

The bartender dropped off his second beer. Luke clamped his fingers around the mug. As he nursed the drink along, a steady trickle of folks filled up the rest of the space between him and the two women and overflowed onto the dance floor. Somebody fed the jukebox in one corner. In another corner, a crowd began to gather around the mechanical bull.

Over the buzz of conversation, Carly's laugh rang out. He'd have recognized it anywhere.

"Sounds as good as she looks," said the guy near him. "You know her?"

"Yeah."

"I wouldn't mind an introduction—"

Luke narrowed his eyes.

"But, uh, I'm not asking," the other man said in a rush. "I can see that would be a waste of my time."

Luke took a long, hard swallow from his mug. Irritation, like the guy to his right, had begun to grate on him. He wanted nothing to do with Carly.

But he needed his job to provide for Rosie and Mom.

Beer mug in hand, he rose from his bar stool.

Time to go make nice with the boss's daughter.

In the Longhorn's ladies' room, Carly sidled past the crowd of chattering women primping at the long counter. She found a spot halfway down the room. But as she stared into the cloudy mirror, she wasn't seeing her reflection.

Instead, she saw Luke the day he had come to the Roughneck years ago.

He'd looked so good in his worn jeans and white shirt, so tanned and fit and strong. For a moment, that overrode her concern at seeing him on the ranch. For another moment, she couldn't fight the tremor of excitement and disbelief running through her. Couldn't tamp down the rush of joy at knowing he was hers.

Only a few days earlier, they had made love for the first time.

Blinking, she looked away from the mirror. As she pulled her hairbrush from her bag, someone touched her back. She moved aside, thinking it was another woman trying get by in the tight space. Instead, the touch came again.

She turned to find Kim close behind her.

"Hey." The women around them made enough noise to cover the sound of a gunshot. Still, Kim stepped closer and muttered, "Let's go for a walk outside."

Carly laughed. "Kim Healy, gangster's moll. What do you want to do, get me out in the parking lot so your boys can fit me up for cement shoes?"

Kim leaned forward and said in a low voice, "Luke's here."

"Is he?" She projected indifference. Heck, she pretended ignorance. The minute they had stepped into the Longhorn, she had seen those unmistakable wide shoulders and that sandy hair. "So?"

"So, I need some air."

Kim led the way out of the room. Instead of going back to the main room, they went down the hall to the emergency exit at the end.

Outside, they walked a few feet along the side of the building. Carly settled on the low stone wall and reached behind it to pick up a couple of pebbles. "The Southwestern landscaping will come in handy for you. Don't you have to fill my pockets with stones?"

"Carly." She didn't need to look to see Kim's worried expression. "What's going on?"

A few yards away, the Longhorn's door swung open. Music and laughter swelled into the night.

As Kim settled on the wall beside her, Carly sighed.

This conversation wasn't going to be to her liking, she could tell.

"Inside," Kim said, "I turned to say something to Sandra, turned back again and you were gone. So I went looking for you. Because you need to talk to me. And I'm done with sitting back and waiting for you to get to that conclusion. That's what's going on. Come on, girl, it's me. Your BFF." She gave Carly a nudge. "You do remember we're best friends forever, right?"

"Yes, I do." Tears made her eyes sting. "I don't know where to start, Kim."

"How about with the week before you and Luke had the fight?"

Now she did turn her head.

In the light of the streetlamp, Kim's set jaw and grim expression matched her flat tone. But the glow in her friend's eyes didn't come from the lamplight.

"You knew something was up?"

Raising her brows, Kim looked at her without speaking.

"Sorry." Carly stared into the distance, where the lights couldn't breach the darkness. "There was a lot going on that week. And then, when Luke and I broke up, I wasn't in the mood to talk about it."

"You fell to pieces," her friend said gently. "You were good for nothing the rest of that summer, till you went away to school. And I'm worried it might happen again."

She snapped her head in Kim's direction. "Don't worry. There's not a chance of that."

"Well, at least at this point, you've only started to crumble around the edges. Just enough for a BFF to notice."

Carly gave a strangled laugh.

"You slept with Luke, didn't you?"

Her breath caught at Kim's outright question. At her spot-on guess. But then, Kim was no dummy and never had been. And Lord only knew, she had probably picked up dozens of clues in that one short week to tell her something momentous had happened in her best friend's life.

Momentous, all right.

Who knew so much could have come from her one and only time with Luke?

Who knew she could have been so naive? So stupid?

"Sorry, Kim. I... It wasn't that I didn't want to tell you back then. I just needed some time." Time to hold her secret excitement close to her heart, the way Luke had held her close to his. "I almost couldn't believe it had happened." She gave a derisive laugh worthy of Brock Baron. "I know that sounds ridiculous, but it's the way I felt."

Special. She'd felt special when she was with Luke. As if she finally stood out from the crowd. Finally meant something to someone who wasn't connected to her by birth or a promise between best friends. "But before I could convince myself it was real...it was over."

"You wouldn't have slept with the guy if you didn't care about him, Carly. And I know how much you did. When you broke up, I let you slide with the excuse you were going off to college and didn't want to get tied down. But I didn't fall for it, even then. What really happened?"

The door to the Longhorn opened. A lone customer turned to go to a motorcycle parked at the opposite end of the building.

Just like that, Luke had turned and walked away from her, too. And, like the customer who revved his engine and tore out of the parking lot, he never looked back.

She swallowed. "I slept with him," she said evenly, flushing with embarrassment over her stupidity but determined to tell Kim the truth. This part of it. "I slept with him, and three days later he showed up on the ranch. My dad was looking for wranglers, and Luke planned to use me to try and get a job at the Roughneck."

"He wouldn't." Kim sounded as stunned as she had felt at the time.

"He would. I confronted him, and he didn't deny it." Despite her struggle to keep her words even, she could hear the strain in her voice. "He didn't even answer me. He just turned and left the ranch."

The door to the Longhorn opened again. A small group of women spilled out of the bar and headed toward them, laughing and lurching and passing them by with farewell waves.

She and Kim waved back.

Another woman trailed behind them, walking steadily and flashing a key ring. "Don't worry. I'm the designated driver."

"Good deal," Kim said.

They sat watching the women make their unsteady way down the length of the building, trailing bursts of screechy laughter behind them. Carly felt grateful for the din. She had more to share with Kim. But not here. Not now. "Time to get back inside." She stood. "We wouldn't want Luke thinking the sight of him scared me away."

"No, we wouldn't."

Carly led the way back to the bar.

She hooked her thumbs into her belt loops. Her stomach felt calm, her nerves steady. She was a woman ready to take on the world—*and* Luke Nobel.

She wasn't at all like the naive teenager of her early college days who had spent weeks in the bathroom of her dorm, dealing with morning sickness.

Chapter Four

Well, dang. Where the heck had the man gone?

Carly clamped her jaw, taking out her frustration on another mint.

Earlier, she had managed to keep track of Luke in the long mirror across from her. Now a slim redhead had taken the stool he had occupied just a minute ago. She leaned back on her own stool and tilted her head, trying to see through the crowd standing three deep behind her.

For all she cared, Luke could be out on the dance floor with some wide-eyed city slicker or snuggled up in a booth with a wannabe buckle bunny. It didn't matter to her what woman had caught his attention or even what the two of them had gotten up to. The important thing was to know exactly where to find him. She didn't want him sneaking up on her. And with her luck, that's just—

"Hey, Carly." Luke's voice rumbled over all the others around them.

She looked up. His reflection stared back at her from the mirror.

He stood directly behind her, the press of the crowd keeping him so close, she would need only to lean back the slightest bit to rest against his broad chest. He could wrap his arms around her and settle his chin on the top of her head, the way he had the night they had curled up on his truck's tailgate to watch the stars come out.

Which had led to their making out.

Which had turned into making love and changed her life forever.

She swiveled on her stool to face him. "What are you doing here, cowboy? I didn't think ranch managers got nights off."

"And I didn't think you'd come back again tonight."

"Back?"

"Yeah, I saw you take off the minute I got up from my stool. You ran like a rodeo clown tearing away from the bull wanting to stomp on his butt."

She laughed and tossed her hair over her shoulder, under cover of checking her surroundings. To her left, Kim sat in conversation with the woman on the other side of her. To the right, she saw only the broad back of the man on the next stool. No chance of interruptions from either of them. No interference, either.

She looked at Luke. "I wouldn't run from a bull. That means I'd have no reason in the world to run from you."

"Good to hear. Buy you a drink?"

She didn't bother to look at her mug. "No, I'm fine, thanks." She swiveled her seat again, deliberately putting her back to him.

He stepped between her stool and Kim's to set his beer mug on the bar. His chest brushed her arm. The rest of him seemed to fill every inch of space between them. The mint between her teeth crunched to bits. She faced forward, which only made things worse. Who the heck was that worried-looking woman in the mirror?

Darn Luke. Maybe Kim hadn't been far off the mark about her falling to pieces. Over the years, she had pulled herself together. But Luke had always had the power to make her feel…not so wild. She had to work twice as hard with him as with anyone else to keep up her pretense. And right now, she desperately needed that defense. She didn't need to sit here with him for the time it would take to share a drink. She didn't want to share that much more of her lifetime with him.

Still, she would never let him see her care.

"So, cowboy…" Her voice sounded much breathier than she'd intended.

As if to hear her better, he lowered his head. Her senses revved into high gear, automatically registering details. The gleam in his light brown eyes. His aftershave, something spicy with a kick to it that made her mouth water. She imagined running her fingertips down the plane of his cheek and along the line of his jaw, could almost feel the gentle scratch of golden five-o'clock shadow.

After what seemed like an eternity, he shifted to lean against the bar. And in a heartbeat, she put her defenses in place again. "So, cowboy." She tried again. "Come here often to pick up women?"

The line wasn't that funny, but he gave her a lopsided smile. "Every chance I get. You interested?"

"I'd rather spend time with that bull over in the corner. In fact, I *plan* to spend time over there."

"With a hunk of metal? That's got nothing on a live bull."

"You'd be surprised."

"I damn sure wouldn't. There's a difference."

"You still need to stay in the saddle."

"True enough." This time, his mouth curved in a full smile.

As far as she could tell, he hadn't moved, but the

space between them suddenly seemed tighter, the air in the room warmer, the lights dimmer.

"You think you can handle it?" he asked.

"I know I can."

"Something besides a slow, sexy ride?"

He had asked the question straight out. No teasing, no taunting, no smile. What else could she expect from a true bull rider? A champion.

Too bad she wasn't in his class.

The question had made her pulse jump to triple time. Her temperature seemed to spike a degree. And her irritation level for even having these reactions put her blood pressure through the roof. "Slow and sexy's for city slickers, and you know it." She leaned forward. In the narrow space, her shirtfront almost brushed his. Giving him the most languid smile she could manage, she added, "I like to make my rides worthwhile."

His eyes lit with his grin. "All right, then." He pointed in the same direction she had. "If you're so confident you have what it takes, why don't you mosey on over there. But if you plan to show me what you've got, you'll really have to crank 'er up."

"Watch me." After all the stories she had told him of her childhood competitions with her brothers, he had to know how she would respond. *Wild and crazy Carly would never pass up a challenge like this one.* Besides, she'd had plenty of experience riding those "hunks of metal" he despised. She'd knock him off his bar stool.

Smiling at the thought, she turned sideways on her own stool. Her knees grazed his champion belt buckle. He sucked in his stomach as if she had zapped him with a cattle prod.

No matter what she'd told Kim, she wasn't immune to Luke. The knowledge bothered her—but at least she had the satisfaction of seeing he wasn't unaffected by her, either.

Still smiling, she went to the small table in one corner of the room. After scribbling her name on the required form, she stood aside to wait her turn.

Luke came up to join her just as a new rider straddled the bull. The crowd pressed forward, eager to watch the show. A man's elbow caught her in the ribs. After a quick "sorry," he turned away again.

From behind her, Luke put a hand on her shoulder. To protect her? To steady her? To keep her still so he could get a better view?

She didn't know and couldn't take the time to care. She was too busy fighting to ignore the heat licking low inside her.

Other riders, two or three or a dozen, took their turns in the saddle. Again, she didn't know and didn't care. Passing up the opportunity to check out their technique might be her downfall in the competition. But she couldn't seem to focus.

When her name was called, Luke squeezed her shoulder lightly. He leaned down, putting his head close to hers again, and murmured, "Have at it, cowgirl."

His voice, deep and intimate, made that lick of heat in her belly flame. But his final word turned the rest of her to ice.

Years ago, she had told Luke her secrets, her longings, her dreams, her fears. Her worries about her place in her family. Her irritation over her dad. She had loved Luke and shared everything with him. Had given him everything, too, the night she'd slept with him.

She had trusted him.

And only days later, he had come to the Roughneck,

as eager to apply for a job there as she'd been to sign up for a ride on this fake bull tonight.

Daddy's little cowgirl, he'd called her that day.

The insult and his desire to work for Brock were the worst forms of betrayal.

Now, she turned and stared at him. He stared back, making her heart skip a beat. She cursed herself for not having better control of her reactions. This man had once done her wrong, no denying it, yet she couldn't keep from responding to him, his nearness, his smile.

"I'll show you a cowgirl, all right," she promised.

I'll show you exactly what Daddy's little girl can do.

And she did.

But the fun she'd once gotten from it had gone.

The ride was rough. She was tilted and jerked around. She fought to go the distance in front of the crowd— because that's what Carly Baron did.

Yet none of it mattered.

Just the way her passion for barrel racing had vanished, so had her interest in riding Luke's "hunk of metal." Was it his scorn over the mechanical substitute that had taken the pleasure from her ride? Would mounting a *real* bull give that feeling back to her?

Or was riding, like her relationship with Luke, just going to be a part of her past?

"So? What do you think?"

Luke shrugged. How the hell had he gotten trapped into this situation?

That brush of Carly's knees against his midsection earlier had just about brought him to *his* knees. This time, he'd stayed two feet away, not wanting to get caught in the crush against her again. The distance didn't help. She had resettled herself on a stool and leaned back to prop her elbows on the bar. The position tugged at the shimmery fabric of her shirt, making it gape just enough to show off a hint of twin curves and the barest edge of lace. Sexy as hell.

Then again, when he looked up, he found her wide blue eyes and full lips just as much of a turn-on. The sight brought him right back to the day he'd met her and seen the shy, insecure girl hiding behind the wild child she'd pretended to be.

She stared at him, her brow crinkled, waiting for his answer, which he would happily provide…as soon as he could recall her question.

After a minute, his brain cells finally kicked in again. She wanted his opinion on her ride. "You cranked the machine up high enough," he said hoarsely. "I'll give you that."

"What about form? I get points for that, too. And, not to mention, for staying in the saddle twice as long as anyone else."

He shrugged. He hadn't been impressed. At least, not by her ride on the bull. Had to admit, though, he'd liked the way her long blond hair tumbled around her shoulders—just the way it had the night they'd made love in the back of his truck.

"Well?" she demanded.

He cleared his throat. "You had some techniques down. I'll throw in points for that, too. But you put about as much of yourself into the ride as Rosie needs to when I cart her around in her little red wagon. As in, none. *Nada.*"

She glared at him. "Who has time for self-expression when they're in the saddle? Besides, bull riding's not an art form."

"Maybe not. But there's a lot more to it than just putting your hands in the right places."

The dim light from the bar couldn't hide the flush that tinged her cheeks. She took a long swallow from the beer he'd bought her.

He wished he'd thought to get another for himself. It had gotten hot in here all of a sudden. With one finger, he loosened his shirt collar. He hadn't intended a double meaning to his words, but man, had he ever hit the bull's-eye with that statement.

Carly had all the right curves and, once upon a time, *his* hands had found all the right places.

The thought immediately registered on another of his body parts. As if she'd read his mind—or seen something he sure as hell didn't want her noticing—she slammed her mug on the bar. "Thanks for the beer."

Before he could blink, she slid from the stool.

Dang.

He dug into his jeans pocket for a few bucks to toss beside her empty mug. Damned near hobbling, he hurried across the room.

She'd already exited through the double doors. Outside, he found her standing at the corner of the building, glaring in the direction of the parking lot.

"Need a ride home?" he asked.

"Got that covered." But she wouldn't look his way.

A sudden suspicion hit him. "Where's your ride?"

She glanced toward a vacant slot close to the edge of the parking area and quickly away again, but he'd already gotten his answer. "You didn't drive, did you? Kim's your ride. And she left a while ago."

"Yeah," she mumbled. "You can bet she's not going to hear the end of that."

"Then I'll take you home. My truck's right here."

He pointed a few spaces away from the vacant slot, to where he'd parked his silver pickup. The same pickup he'd owned since high school, which meant she more than likely recognized it.

"No, thanks. I'll find another ride."

"Why bother? It's not like driving you home takes me out of my way." He lived on the ranch in the manager's quarters, within a stone's throw of the main house. She didn't respond, and he swallowed a curse. "Carly, for crying out loud. Whatever happened in the past shouldn't keep us from spending a few minutes in the truck together."

Yet, damn, even as she stood there glaring at him, he thought of the many times they had made out in the front seat of that very same truck. Again, he recalled what they'd done in the back of it. Exactly what he wanted to do now.

He ran his hand inside his shirt collar. Hell, it was hot out here, too.

Maybe she had the right idea. Maybe he should call a cab to come and get her.

She hiked the strap of her purse over her shoulder, then winced. Not in dislike or disgust but in pain.

"You okay?" Genuine concern made him ask. Still, he couldn't ignore the sinking feeling in the pit of his stomach. This would be all he needed, to have Brock Baron's little girl hurt the minute he was alone with her. Worse, to be the one to *have gotten* Brock Baron's little girl hurt. "What's wrong?"

"Nothing."

"Dammit, Carly. I saw your face when you dismounted from that bull. Ever since, you've favored your right arm. Did you hurt yourself on the ride?"

She shook her head. "No, it's nothing. Just an old racing injury. It flares up once in a while."

He'd be willing to bet she hadn't said a word to her family about the spill. If she had, he'd already have heard about it from one of the Baron men—if not from her brother, Jet, then from one of her stepbrothers. For sure, from Jacob, who lived and breathed rodeo the way he himself once had. "What's the time frame on this 'old' injury?"

She shrugged—using her good shoulder. "About a month."

He bit back a curse. "What happened?"

"Nothing exciting. I was practicing the barrels, coming in close, and dropped my hand too soon. The mare wanted to shoulder, and I wasn't ready. I just wasn't with it at all that day. And I paid for it. I went flying and landed on my arm."

"Hard, I'd wager."

"Yes, but I'm fine. It only gives me trouble once in a while."

"Where does it hurt?"

"Luke. Really. It's not even my arm, only my shoulder."

"Have you had any therapy for it?"

She shook her head. "Give it up, will you, please? I told you, I'm fine. I won't feel a thing in the morning."

If only he could say the same. Chances were, his meeting with her tonight would have him hungover from a long night of little sleep.

No point in continuing this argument about her injury. Just like when he worked with a skittish mare, the more he would talk, the more she would balk. With the mare, he'd put in the time and summon the patience to calm her down, to get her comfortable with him. To get the job done.

With Carly, he'd be a fool to push the issue when he ought to be stepping away as fast as he could. "Come on, then. Let's get home."

To CARLY'S RELIEF, Luke did give his questioning a rest—at least, until they'd reached Roughneck Ranch.

When he had said he would take her home, she hadn't known he'd meant *his* home. To her dismay, he pulled up behind the small single-story ranch house and turned off the truck's engine.

Then he started in on her again.

"Do your folks know about your fall?"

"No," she snapped. "There was no need to tell them. There still isn't." Before he could say another word, she exited the truck and slammed the door behind her. The fixture over the back porch illuminated a good part of the yard. It certainly gave off enough light for her to see his disgruntled expression through the windshield.

A second later, he slammed his door closed, too. "You know, Carly, there's a difference between being independent and being too danged stubborn to listen to reason."

"That's not your worry."

He exhaled in disgust. "And you always were the most bullheaded critter I knew."

"Takes one to know one, I say."

"Luke?"

She jumped. The voice had come from the direction of the porch. A woman stood framed in the kitchen doorway, looking out at them through the screen door.

"I thought I heard the truck. And voices." The woman smiled at them. "Everything all right out here?"

"Just fine, Mom."

Luke's mother. Of course. She had never met the woman but could easily have guessed her relationship to Luke. He had lighter brown eyes than his mother's, but they shared the same sandy-blond shade of hair.

He had once told her he had never felt lost in a crowd at home, the way she had when she was growing up. His mom was his only family—or had been, until he had married…and his wife had had their child.

With a twinge of guilt, Carly thought of the doors they had closed much too hard and the voices they had raised too high. "Sorry if we disturbed you."

"No trouble. I was just coming into the kitchen after getting Rosie tucked up—again. Let's not stand out here. Come on in." His mother swung the door wide.

"Thanks, but—"

"Yes," Luke said, "let's go inside."

Before she could continue with her trumped-up excuse, he moved closer and took her elbow. Her good elbow.

He knew darned well she had been about to turn down his mother's invitation.

Before she could pull away, he stepped forward, urging her toward the house. Like a calf snared by a well-aimed lasso, she had no choice but to follow along.

Chapter Five

Carly knew Luke's house almost as well as he did himself.

For the past couple of years, once she'd heard Luke had moved onto the ranch, she had made sure her brief visits home hadn't taken her anywhere near the place. But as a child, she'd visited here many times, tagging along like Brock's shadow when he had needed to stop in to see the previous ranch manager.

A quick glance around the kitchen told her nothing much had changed since then.

"Uhh…Mom, this is Carly Baron. Carly, my mom, Tammy."

The woman laughed. "No introductions necessary for me, Luke. I'd know this girl anywhere. I've seen her picture often enough over at the house. It's a pleasure meeting you at last, Carly."

"Same here, Mrs. Nobel."

"Call me Tammy. I've heard so much about you from Anna and Julieta and your sisters, I feel as though I know you already. They're thrilled to have you back here."

Luke had said something like that the day they'd met again. And Carly fell back on her automatic response. "Just for a while," she murmured.

"I'm sure they're all hoping for more than that."

Tammy smiled. "There's nothing like living close to family."

"I don't know, Mom," Luke said. "Sometimes, I wonder if you regret not moving to San Antonio when you had the chance."

"And leave my only granddaughter?" Tammy opened her eyes wide, teasing him. At the moment, she didn't look much older than Luke.

"Ah," he said. "So, Rosie's the only draw here?"

"I'd say 'on some days,' but you'd know better." After giving him an affectionate smile, she turned her attention back to Carly. "Can I get you something before I go?"

And leave me with Luke? "No, I'm fine. In fact, I'll let you two—"

"Stay for a minute, Carly," Luke interrupted. "I'll just walk Mom out."

Both his words and the flash of interest in his mother's face made her tense up again.

Tammy only glanced from her to Luke and back. Smiling, she said, "I'll look forward to seeing you again soon."

"I will, too." Carly forced a smile. So polite. So civilized. So heartbreaking, when at one time she had dreamed of having this woman welcome her into Luke's family.

"Go on ahead into the living room." He gestured toward the kitchen doorway. "The seating's more comfortable in there."

She didn't want to sit in the living room or anywhere else in this house.

She also didn't want to make a scene in front of his mother. Who knew what Tammy already thought about Luke walking in here with his boss's daughter? Or how quickly she would carry tales over to the main house when she visited?

"Good night," Carly said.

As the woman gathered her bags from the kitchen table, Carly slipped through the doorway. One glance across the room she had entered left her feeling as if a bull had found *his* comfortable seating on her chest.

From behind her, she could hear Luke and his mother talking. They hadn't left the kitchen. For her, there was no safe return.

She barely noted the sound of the back door closing, cutting off Tammy's voice.

She crossed the living room to the couch and sank onto it. When she set her hands flat on either side of her, the nubby fabric tickled her palms. She licked her suddenly dry lips.

The kitchen might not have changed much, but she had never seen this room the way it looked now.

"Carly?"

At the sound of Luke's voice, she jumped. She hadn't heard his approach. He stood in the doorway, his broad shoulders filling most of the frame. Just as she had dreaded, she was alone in this house with Luke....

Except for the little girl down the hall.

As if he'd read her mind, he said, "Let me go check on Rosie, make sure she's still tucked in. Mom said she's restless and on the cranky side tonight."

He went down the short hallway leading to the bedrooms and bathroom.

She hadn't wanted to come here with Luke to begin with. Now was her chance to go. Too bad it wasn't time for her to leave the ranch altogether.

Sadly, she thought of the first time she had left, to go to school in Houston. After graduation, she had stayed there, thinking it would help her forget Luke. But that hadn't worked. Nothing had, especially once she had discovered she was carrying his child.

She hadn't done very well, either, with the idea of remaining in Houston to gain independence from her family. Of finding where she belonged. No matter how much distance she put between herself and the Roughneck, she couldn't stay away. Not forever.

As the past few years had taught her, nothing could keep her from loving her family. Just as nothing could help her forget what she had once shared with Luke.

Sitting here in his living room only made her loss more poignant.

In front of her, children's picture books covered one long edge of the coffee table, so neatly aligned it was clear someone besides a two-year-old had last touched them. Tammy must have taken the time to arrange the books. Or maybe Luke had straightened them.

In one corner of the room sat a stack of toys. Some of them triggered faint memories from her own childhood.

From another corner, a pile of stuffed animals stared at her, their shiny plastic eyes unblinking, their cloth smiles firmly in place. The animals littered the carpet in that area, as if neither Luke nor his mother had the heart to corral them.

With her first glance from the living room doorway, she had seen a couple of curio cabinets sitting directly opposite the couch. Now she looked more closely at the cabinets and the wall around them. Everywhere, she saw picture frames, an endless series of photos, shots of Luke, his mother, his wife. And his little girl.

The photos showed every stage of his daughter's development, beginning with a picture of her as a just-born baby wrapped in a soft pink blanket. In an oversize photo on the center shelf of one of the cabinets, the child stood behind a birthday cake decorated with a candle in the shape of the number two. The photo must have been taken only a month or so earlier. The child could probably come down the hall from her bedroom right this minute and look as if she'd stepped from the frame.

In every photo, Luke smiled at his little girl, a miniature version of himself who shared his hair color and had the same warm-honey eyes. The look of love and pride on his face made her heart ache.

She should have shelves of photos of her own. She should be feeling that love and pride. She should have a child now.

Hers and Luke's.

Tears stung her eyes. She rested her hand on her stomach. It was flat now, but once it had been swollen from the baby she'd carried.

"Are you okay?"

She jumped. Again. Luke stood a few yards away from her, a towel tossed over one shoulder. Just as at the Longhorn's bar, the space around her seemed to close in.

"I'm fine." She rose from the couch. She began to shove her hands into her back pockets, winced as pain shot through her shoulder and thought better of the idea.

"You sure?" he asked. "You seem out of it."

"I'm just…tired."

"You were looking at the wall of fame. My daughter's life in pictures."

His smile made her eyes sting again. His words made her heart ache. She couldn't talk about his baby. But she had to get through this conversation without letting him suspect she had something to hide. "She's a pretty little girl."

His smile widened to a grin that left her weak-kneed and wishing she'd stayed on the couch.

"I'll accept that as a compliment. Mom says she takes after me more than she does my wife. You remember Jodi."

She would never forget Jodi.

How could she, when Luke had begun dating the other girl so soon after they had split up. Learning that news had given her another reason to stay in Houston. Later, his marriage had only increased her desire to postpone any trips home.

"She was a couple of years ahead of me in school. But, yes, I remember her. From the cheering squad." From the head cheerleader position, to be exact. The petite brunette with the perky ponytail had always made Carly, two years younger, feel as big as one of her brothers. In the photos, Jodi barely reached Luke's well-developed biceps.

"You heard what happened?"

"Yes." Jodi's obsession over show jumping equaled the love Carly had once felt for barrel racing. During a competition, Jodi's horse had thrown her. She had hit her head and, despite wearing a helmet, had suffered brain trauma that led to a coma. She didn't recover. Savannah had told her the news the next time Carly had come home for a visit...when she had also learned Luke had been hired as the Roughneck's ranch manager.

"I'm sorry for your loss." She stumbled over the standard phrase, wanting to say so much more.

I'm sorry for the loss of your wife and the loss of our baby and for never even letting you know you were going to be a daddy.

His expression had gone blank, as if he had shut off his emotions. "I can't imagine what it will be like for

Rosie to grow up without knowing Jodi." He eyed her. "You'd know, wouldn't you? Although, at least you have some memories of your mama before she left. And your stepmom before she died."

The words made her breath catch. After everything he'd gone through, and after all these years, he still remembered. She had told him about being abandoned as a child and, later, losing the stepmother she had just come to love.

But of course he would remember. He worked here on the ranch now, saw her family every day, and got along well with Jet and her stepbrothers, especially Jacob.

"Sometimes I think it'd be easier not to have any memories," she admitted.

"I guess that's true for a lot of life. But we don't always get to do things the easy way, do we?"

He stepped closer. She stiffened so abruptly, pain from her shoulder shot down her arm. She didn't know where he intended to go with that statement. She didn't want to know why he kept walking toward her with that unreadable look on his face. Now was no time for a cozy chat about their past, if that was what he had in mind.

But when he halted in front of her, he said nothing, just stood looking down at her. She refused to look up. Instead, she watched his Adam's apple move when he swallowed hard, then his shirtfront rise and fall with one heavy, sighing breath.

Time ticked on, until she couldn't take the silence any longer. Couldn't handle the suspense.

She glanced up. He was so close. Just as when they had talked at the bar, she would only need to lean forward to make contact with him.

She had been playing the wild girl then—or trying to—but inside, she'd felt too chicken to do what she'd wanted. To reach out and touch him. Now, she longed to do more than that, to kiss him and run her fingers through his hair and pretend she was eighteen years old again....

He looked as though he might have thoughts about returning to the past, too. But there was no way they could go back to the place...to the people...they were before.

Ruthlessly, she pushed aside her memories and desires, feeling too aware of all those baby photos staring at them, too conscious of his daughter sleeping just a few rooms away. Too troubled by the secret she couldn't share.

Darn Luke.

She should have left here the moment she had gotten out of his truck. And she would have, if he hadn't pulled up close enough to the back porch for Tammy to overhear them and come to the kitchen door. Well, Tammy was gone. She took a step back. "Time for me to get home."

"I don't think so." He smiled. "Take off your shirt."

LUKE WOULD HAVE given next week's pay for a photo of Carly at that moment. He'd never seen her eyes open that wide or her face turn such an interesting shade of red.

Before she could explode, he said, "Hang on. I'm not propositioning you. That shoulder of yours needs some attention, and you're getting it from me."

"Are you out of your mind?"

"Can you reach where it hurts?"

"What does that matter?" she demanded. "You can't possibly think you're—"

"What I think is, you're sure as hell not going to get anyone at the main house to rub you down. Because you're not going to tell them you're injured. Are you?"

When she said nothing, he held up the jar of ointment

he had taken from the bathroom cabinet. "I thought not. So I'll ask you again, can you reach?"

"No. But I don't need to put anything on my shoulder."

"Carly. What are you afraid of?"

"Nothing."

"Then prove it. It's not like you've got something I've never seen. Or never touched." He raised the jar to her eye level. "Come on. It'll be harmless." Even as he said the word, a sliver of doubt stabbed him. Touching Carly could never be harmless.

Somehow, he would have to find a way to forget about his craving. He'd focus instead on his guilt over goading her into riding that bull.

She didn't need to say a word. Her wrinkled brow, narrowed eyes and tight lips all shouted her reluctance to have him touch her. But the fact she hadn't punched him or run screaming from the room told him she was hurting more than she wanted to admit. He moved in for the verbal kill. "If you're planning to push your daddy around in his wheelchair, the last thing you want is to be sidelined by a frozen shoulder."

That got her.

She took a deep breath and let it out in a sigh. "Okay. Fine. Turn around."

He laughed. "That's my line, isn't it? How do you expect me to reach you from that position?"

"Turn around."

Smiling, he obeyed, looking toward the curio cabinet across the room. How would she take it if she knew the cabinet's mirrored interior showed her reflection as she unbuttoned her flashy shirt?

Probably not well at all.

Nice as the view might have been, he tore his gaze away. No worries. His memories replaced the real-time vision with another guaranteed to keep him satisfied: the sight of Carly kneeling with him on the blanket-lined bed of his truck, allowing *him* the pleasure of taking off her shirt.

"All right."

The words startled him back to the present.

He turned to her, the jar of ointment clutched tight.

She held her unbuttoned shirt together in front of her. A lacy pink bra peeked out from beneath one edge of the fabric. The scent of perfume wafted from her warmed skin. A softness around her mouth said she might be recalling that night in the truck, too.

A hard weight suddenly pressed against his zipper.

"Yeah." He swallowed. "Okay, your turn." He gestured for her to face away from him.

She had taken her right arm out of the sleeve and left the fabric draped over her shoulder. He swallowed again, harder this time. Then he reached out to slide the blouse away, revealing lightly tanned skin just as perfect as it had been when she was a teen. He could already feel the smoothness.

As he opened the jar, his hands shook. "This'll be cold at first," he warned.

She reached up to sweep her hair across her good shoulder. "Just get it over with. Please."

Seconds after he touched her, he found himself in trouble. Big trouble. His fingertips tingled, and not solely from the ointment. Almost subconsciously, he shuffled forward, telling himself he needed a better angle. A hell of a lie there, for someone who prided himself on his truthfulness. But concern about her shoulder had retreated to somewhere in the back of his mind, taken over by the pure excitement of being near her again. By the desire to get even closer.

As he rubbed the cream over the curve of her shoulder, she tilted her head, exposing the side of her neck. His own experiences gave him the reason for her movement. Chances were, after all this time with an untreated injury, the pain had traveled. And damn, his hands wanted to travel, too, over every curve and—

Right. As if he didn't have enough problems. Swallowing a curse, he forced himself to focus. "Having trouble with your neck, too?"

"Some."

He moved his hand slowly along the muscle from her shoulder to the base of her head. Her low moan vibrated deep inside him.

"Feel good?" he murmured.

"Mmm."

His fingertips grazed her hair. He fought to keep from sliding his hand across her other shoulder, down through the mass of blond waves and around a generous curve of pink lace. After a deep, steadying breath, he said, "You probably should've had therapy right after your fall." She said nothing. She would never admit he was right. "Have you had anyone at all treating this shoulder for you?"

"No."

At her admission, he had a sudden, hopeful thought.

Carly had been the most beautiful girl he'd ever seen, bar none, and her looks had only gotten better over time. In the years they'd been apart, there wasn't a chance in hell that someone this hot had never dated. Had never had another lover.

But he wanted to believe that, since her fall a month earlier, he was the only man who had touched her like this.

He cupped his hand on the back of her neck. She

turned her head, all the invitation—or all the excuse—he needed to move around to stand in front of her.

With his thumb, he massaged her neck and watched as her blue eyes began to glisten. The tense set of her shoulders said she was reining herself in, trying not to respond. But the gleam in her eyes and the look on her face told him another story. He'd seen that expression earlier tonight, too, when they'd stood close together in the crush at the saloon.

Hell, he'd caught that same look on his own face in the mirror over the bar.

When they had left the Longhorn, getting this close to Carly again had been the very last thing he'd wanted.

Now, it was all he could think about.

"What happened to harmless?" she whispered.

"You happened." He smiled. "No problem with a little kiss, is there?"

"A little kiss," she repeated. Her eyes narrowed. "And then what? We just go back to where we left off that summer we were together?"

He stiffened but managed to keep his hand resting lightly on the back of her neck. He rubbed that tight muscle again. "No. We can't go back. We're different people now."

"What makes you so sure you want to kiss the woman I turned out to be?" She tried to toss off the question, but her voice shook.

Going with his first thought would probably get him slapped. He opted for the second. "Maybe that's part of starting fresh and going forward."

"You wish."

He smiled. "The act's not working."

"Neither is your seduction…if that's what this is."

Frowning, he took his hand from her neck. "What the hell—?"

"Now I think it's really time for me to go. But I'll need to be prepared. What did you say to your mother?"

"Huh? What did I say about what?"

"Me." She cleared her throat. "Us."

"Just that we met at the Longhorn and I gave you a ride back to the ranch."

Dead silence.

He tried again. "If you mean 'us' from years ago, I never said anything to anyone. You asked me not to, remember?" He didn't have to think hard to recall that day or how her face had looked when she'd made that request.

Emotionless. Empty.

Just the way he had felt at hearing it.

"You didn't want anyone to find out I even knew you." He'd gone through that before, time and time again. As a kid and as a teen. With folks he'd once called his friends.

"It wasn't that—"

"It was. And it seems like you still care only about what someone else would think. I can't say you've got the wrong idea." Finally coming to his senses, he stepped back an arm's length from her, shaking his head. Maybe the distance would keep him from acting like a fool again.

Carly might wonder what his mom would think. He had a lot more than that to concern him. He had both his mother and his daughter to care for. *And* Carly's father to worry about.

Forget getting fired. That would be only the first of a long list of his troubles.

Brock Baron's influence spread the length and breadth of Texas and far beyond. Crossing a boss who held that much power could get a man blacklisted from ranching.

Could have him working a pipeline in Alaska, nowhere near his mother or child.

"You're right," he said. "This was a bad idea. It wouldn't be harmless at all."

"No, it wouldn't." She looked away. "And we've already got enough regrets."

Chapter Six

After taking a helluva long time to get to sleep, Luke woke up feeling like a new man again, forgetting all about his conversation with Carly. Forgetting what it had felt like to be so close to her again...

Well, all right, maybe he hadn't forgotten what had happened last evening. But by this morning, he had gotten himself back on track again and put his priorities in order.

"You ready for a walk, Rosie?"

He lifted his daughter from the carrier in the backseat of his truck and settled her hat more firmly around her ears.

"Pftt," she said, grabbing the brim of his Stetson.

"Yeah, I know. You'd rather have a hat like Daddy's. But yours is even better for keeping you covered from the sun."

Though that sun was still low in the sky, he wasn't taking any chances with his girl. "Hang in there. We'll only be out here for a few minutes. Just long enough for Daddy to check the fencing."

Rosie settled in his arms. He stood there for a minute, watching her take in their surroundings. They were only a couple of miles from the main ranch house on the Roughneck. Still, there wasn't much in view nearby but dry scrub and drier land. A long fence line guarded the edge of an arroyo. And, off in the distance, a range of mountains, like a row of guards themselves, stood shoulder to shoulder to wait for that rising sun.

It always amazed him to see how Rosie observed a new environment, gazing around as if everything she saw was yet another new miracle.

She was the miracle in his world, the one who made his life worth living. How he'd ever gotten along without her, he would never know.

He gave her a quick hug as he carried her closer to the fence line to make his inspection.

Recent heavy rains from the west had washed away a chunk of soil already loosened by a few of the more curious calves. "My boys were right to report this, Rosie. We need to get the fence fixed. We don't want the animals getting caught in here, do we?" The gap was big enough to trap any calves who might feel even more adventurous.

And, dang it, that thought brought Carly to the front of his mind again. "Some animals just like doing things in their own way. Some people, too. Like Carly Baron." Carly had sure nailed it when she'd talked about never liking to do the expected. Just one of the things that had attracted him to her—and it had been the start of a long, long list.

Judging by the way his stomach had flipped when he'd set eyes on her again less than a week ago, for the first time in years, that attraction hadn't lessened any.

His bad luck.

"You haven't had the pleasure of meeting Carly yet, have you? Though I'm not positive how much of a pleasure it would be."

Rosie laughed. She couldn't have picked up on his

ironic tone. She didn't know what all the words meant. She just liked hearing his voice. So he talked.

"Now, you listen to me. When you grow up, don't you be getting crazy ideas in your head." Going off to earn a college degree was one thing. He still couldn't understand how Carly could have stayed in Houston and not come home.

He strapped Rosie into her carrier again and tapped her gently on the nose. "You stick with your ol' daddy and don't go running off, you hear?"

The way Carly had.

Knowing she could take care of herself, she called it.

I learned how to live on my own. That's something no one can take away from me.

Now, that statement he sure could argue with her over. That day at the barbecue, he'd let it go. Just as he had when she'd made an attempt to pick a fight by tossing her accusation at him.

You don't need to make nice with the boss's daughter.

"Make nice, well, hel—" He cut himself short—too late—and shook his head. "Sorry, baby. Daddy told you he'd work on not using that language around you, didn't he?"

Rosie grinned up at him. She was very forgiving.

Not like Carly Baron, who would never forget what had happened the last time they'd seen each other years ago.

He U-turned the truck, jouncing across the uneven land, making Rosie giggle.

After a while, he could see civilization again—the arena Brock had set up on the ranch, where he and his family kept up their rodeo skills. The barns and outbuildings. The ranch house. And, farther along, the small house he and Rosie shared, where Tammy would be waiting to take over babysitting duties so he could get to work.

If he had some good luck, he wouldn't cross paths again with Carly, who would also never forgive what she thought he had done to her years ago. Back then, she hadn't bothered to ask him about his intentions before lobbing her accusation at him.

That was one thing he had to give her credit for— being able to hit him where it hurt without his seeing it coming.

Not anymore, though. He wouldn't go anywhere near Carly without having his eyes wide-open.

Even better, he wouldn't go anywhere near Carly at all.

A HUNK OF METAL had nothing on a real, live, stinkin', snortin', stompin' bull.

Heart in her throat, Carly fought to keep her butt where it belonged. The animal her brothers used for practice wasn't having any of that idea. Her hundred-twenty-plus pounds in jeans and sturdy boots were no match for twelve hundred pounds of playful bull.

Twister flicked his heavy haunches and tossed her as easily as Anna tossed greens for a salad. Carly landed in the dust of the arena, splat, like a thrown tomato. Again.

The hands she'd convinced to clown for her got Twister a safe distance away. To her embarrassment, it took her longer than the past several times to haul herself over the top rail of the fence.

She hadn't been kidding when she'd told Savannah she was getting soft sitting around the ranch house. After today's short session with Twister, every muscle in her body seemed stretched like a worn-out rubber band. Worse, every bone felt as though it had been worked over with an off-duty branding iron.

Once she dropped down from the fence, her aches and pains dropped, too...all the way to the bottom of her worry list.

Not ten yards away, her father sat staring at her from one of the ranch's ATVs.

Lord help us all, he's mobile was her first thought. *And I'm not* came immediately after.

She clamped her jaw tight and did her best to walk forward without limping—or whimpering—from the pain.

"Carly, what the hell are you doing?" Brock shouted.

Pal, the horse she'd ridden out to the arena earlier, stood beside the rail. His ears twitched at the sound of Brock's roar. She patted the horse's flank and wished she could just as easily calm her dad.

The ranch hand in the driver's seat beside him shifted and glanced away, looking as if he wanted to disappear. It reminded her of what she had said to Luke the afternoon she'd first run into him again. She hadn't disappeared in a puff of smoke. Right now, she very much wished she could.

"I'm practicing."

"Looking to get yourself killed, you mean."

"Not by Twister, Daddy. He's gotten too tame to be homicidal." Beside her, Pal nickered, as if in agreement. "I'm surprised the boys get any good workouts from him."

Brock's snort was worthy of one from Twister. "Don't give me that. I saw how that tame bull tossed you off."

"I just had a bad ride."

"You'll have a bad life if you don't take more care. You've got a couple of cowhands who know next to nothing playing clown for you and nobody else around."

Darn Jet. When he hadn't been able to make it out

here to the arena on Saturday, she had practiced on her own. But he had said he would show up today. Where was he?

"I'm fine, Daddy." *As long as I don't move.* She had started with a sore shoulder. Now the rest of her body had caught up to match it. "You don't need to worry about me and my pastimes."

His eyes narrowed. "That attitude is just what's going to get you into hot water."

"Trouble's my middle name. Didn't you always tell me so?"

"Dammit, Carly. If you're going to be crazy enough to ride bulls, you need to take some precautions."

"I am. I'm wearing a helmet." She held it up by the strap. "And you know getting thrown is just part of the ride."

On the rough track beyond the arena, a battered silver pickup truck approached. She didn't need to see the driver's face to know who sat behind the wheel. Automatically, she stood straighter, fighting a wave of another kind of pain.

Brock had seen the truck, too. He gave a piercing whistle and waved his Stetson. The driver turned in their direction.

The last thing she wanted was Luke Nobel and Brock Baron with her at the same time. Her dad would get ideas, if he didn't have them already. Even now, she didn't like the contemplative look in his eyes.

And she didn't want to see Luke's eyes again.

He had parked the truck and leaned into the backseat, giving her a good view of jeans stretched tight enough to make her heart trip. Once, she had loved his broad shoulders, but that didn't mean she hadn't been equally enthralled by that nice rear end.

What the heck was she doing thinking about Luke like that?

She'd had her chance to get closer to him last night. And she'd almost taken that opportunity. Almost grabbed it—and him—with both hands.

Thank heaven she'd come to her senses and gotten out of there. Then why did she suddenly feel regret, when she'd done the right thing, the only thing possible for her to do?

Luke ambled across the short space, one hand touching the brim of his Stetson in acknowledgement of a lady's presence.

Or more likely, of his boss in the vicinity.

"Morning. You waved me down, Brock. Something we need to discuss?"

"A list," her dad said shortly. "Carly's out here on her own—"

"But not for long," she cut in. "I'm going to head out. I've got to go over to the Peach Pit. I'll leave you to discuss ranch business with…your manager."

She mounted Pal and grimaced as she landed in the saddle. Everything hurt. Including her pride. Brock couldn't have made his lack of faith in her plainer, and she didn't want him chewing her out in front of Luke. "I'll see you back at the house later."

She took off without a care that urging Pal into a gallop would only worsen the pain. Without having a single thought except getting distance from the men behind her.

CARLY ON HORSEBACK, her blond hair streaming behind her, was a sight to behold. Luke took his fill of it…until he caught Brock eyeing him.

He forced his mind to business. "I've just been out taking a look at that fence line Wes told us about. We'll need to reinforce all through that area. I've already moved the herd temporarily to the upland pasture."

The boss nodded without comment, seeming distracted. He sat alone in the ATV, having sent his designated driver over to help the hands at the arena.

"That section of fencing was next on the rotation, anyhow. We'll wrap up and move on in the next day or two."

Luke waited but still Brock said nothing. Unusual for him, especially lately. Though he was always hands-on when it came to the ranch, his circumstances now had given him the time to get even more involved. Since his accident, the boss had also grown broody and short-tempered, which Luke attributed to the man's broken leg and enforced immobility.

After another minute of silence, he went over to his truck. Sooner or later, Brock would come out of his deep thoughts and then a list of orders would be sure to come his way.

Or a chewing out.

The boss hadn't said a word about it yet, but at the barbecue last week, Luke had seen the man eyeing him when he'd sat at the picnic table talking to Carly. Maybe the boss hadn't liked what he'd viewed as Luke hitting on his little girl.

He carried Rosie over to the ATV, rested his foot securely on the running board and set her on his knee.

"Bok!" she blurted, clapping her hands.

Luke grinned. She loved the boss, and the feeling always seemed mutual.

Brock chucked her under the chin. "This is a sweet one you've got here."

"I know it," Luke said. "And she's getting cuter by the day, if I have to say it myself. But I'll admit, she's also turning into a handful."

"Daughters will do that, all right," Brock said dryly. "You'll be in for a rude awakening down the line if you don't get a handle on this girl of yours now."

"I'm trying." He swallowed a smile. In a rare moment, the boss might moan and groan about one of his kids, but he'd move heaven and the entire state of Texas for any of them, if necessary. Just as *he* would for Rosie.

This was a first, though, getting parenting tips from Brock Baron.

Not that he minded help from any source. This single-dad business took a lot out of a man. But when his life had changed two years ago, drastically and without warning, he'd made his decisions and never looked back. The man sitting inches from him now had played a big role in that.

If not for this job managing Roughneck Ranch, Luke didn't know where he'd be. Chances were good he wouldn't have the luxury of tucking his baby into her crib every night.

"That girl of mine…"

Luke eyed the boss warily. The look on his face didn't bode well. Was it time for the chewing out he'd expected? Or worse?

"What are you doing with your spare time?" Brock asked suddenly.

Damn. Was this about the Longhorn? He'd fess up if it came down to it, but meanwhile, he'd hope like hell it wouldn't. "I spend some of it helping my mom when she needs it. But Rosie's my top priority. She takes up most of the rest of my time."

"I need to appropriate some of it."

"Well, sure, if there's something you need done."

"Carly's looking to get into bull riding," Brock said. "I want you to help her out."

Luke rubbed his chin. He prayed the boss hadn't seen the way his jaw had dropped before he'd found the wits to clamp his mouth shut again.

He didn't want to be around Carly. He had to convince the man his request was a bad idea. "I haven't been on a bull in a long while."

"You've had a hard time of things these past couple of years, especially considering all the adjustments you've made." They both knew those adjustments included giving up rodeo. "But no matter what, nobody can take away the fact you're the best bull rider around."

Though the words warmed him, especially coming from Brock Baron, he shook his head. "I did all right. I'd never make it if I tried getting back into rodeo today."

Brock waved a hand, brushing the comment away. "That skill doesn't leave when you're a natural, son. You'd get back up to speed in no time. And you've still got the know-how. The all-important techniques. And," he ended flatly, "I need your expertise."

"I'd like to help, Brock. But with Rosie here keeping me busy, and helping my mom, I haven't got the spare time."

"That doesn't matter. Free time. Work time. I don't care when you do it. Just do it." He had turned as cranky as Rosie when she missed a nap.

The boss's request had turned into an order.

And as Carly wouldn't hesitate to tell him, he took orders from the boss.

"You want me to help her here, at the ranch?"

"Yes. Right here. For as long as she's in town."

Luke glanced over at the arena. He would have given an eyetooth, as the saying went, to have had access to it back in the days when it would've done him some good. Now, it wasn't a job perk he needed.

Just as he sure as hell didn't need this enforced involvement with Carly.

Rosie squirmed on his knee. He lifted her up to his shoulder so she could inspect the area.

The boss grimaced. "That daughter of mine likes to do things her own way," he said, unknowingly echoing what Luke had told Rosie just a short while ago. "I doubt very much she'll take advice from any of her brothers, and she certainly won't want it from me. That doesn't matter, anyhow. As I said, you're the best. If she's determined to go through with the idea, you're the one I want training her. She can hardly take exception to getting tips from a champ."

"Former champ," he said. But the words were drowned out by Rosie's squeal. She was getting restless, and that would give him a reason to leave, to take her home. To figure out how the heck he could get out of this deal.

He put Rosie back into her car seat, then returned to Brock. "I'll be over at the barn after I get Rosie settled with Mom."

Brock nodded.

The boss's demand had thrown him as hard as he'd ever been tossed from the back of a bull.

He didn't want to help Carly out, with bull riding or anything else. Didn't want to get that close to her again. Didn't want another chance to look into those pretty blue eyes or see her scattering of freckles or her soft, pink mouth and—

Hell's bells. He was getting turned on by the boss's daughter—right in front of the boss.

He nodded a farewell and walked away, trying to ease his clamped jaw. He'd be a lot better off if he never saw Carly Baron again.

Not gonna be an option.

Worse, he could already see the way things would go if he refused to help Brock's baby girl.

Carly would do what it took to get back at him, the number-one choice being telling her daddy Luke had slept with her.

And Brock Baron would fire him—right after he had him gelded.

Chapter Seven

The next afternoon, Brock's crankiness reached an all-time high.

Carly didn't pay much attention to the behind-the-scenes operations of Baron Energies, but according to Julieta and Lizzie, something was up. Something connected to the merger proposal the company had received a couple of months ago. Back then, they should have known better than to try to keep the information from their resident invalid, who had eventually gotten word of the situation.

This new development had put him in a foul mood.

She didn't care to ask about whatever was going on. She darn sure didn't want to draw his fire about the fact she'd refused to work for him.

But she felt grateful the incident had taken his mind from their meeting at the arena the day before.

He'd kept her busy all day long, running through pages of memos and letters and directives to his staff, and she appreciated that, too. It kept her too distracted to think of Luke.

Late in the afternoon, she plopped a stack of folders onto the edge of the desk and looked at Brock, who sat behind the desk in his wheelchair. "If we're done with this batch, I'm going to take a ride."

"Out at the arena?" he asked.

She shook her head. "No, I meant in the truck. I think I'll run over to the Peach Pit and see if Savannah could use a hand. See you later." After a quick farewell wave, she left the room.

His question about the arena made her wonder just what he had said to Luke after she left yesterday. But, as with the situation at Baron Energies, she wasn't about to ask.

She wished she could close off her mind as well as she was closing her mouth. She hadn't had many spare seconds at all today, but with every one, her thoughts had turned to Luke.

She had come much too close to letting him kiss her Monday night. Worse, before that point in their evening, she had already fought the temptation to lean closer and kiss him.

What a fool.

How could she be so stupid as to want Luke when he didn't want her? Hadn't she learned anything since the day he'd walked away from her?

She would never forget that day. The wranglers had all been out working the ranch. She had headed to the barn to saddle up Pal for a ride and stopped in shock at seeing Luke's truck.

When he told her he had come to interview for a job with her daddy, she'd felt the blood drain from her face. He hated his job at the gas station and often talked about finding something better, always swearing he would do something to get ahead.

Something like making friends with her?

"Is this your way of getting up in the world?" she managed.

He didn't seem to notice her lack of enthusiasm. "Yeah.

A grease monkey isn't exactly the best match for Daddy's little cowgirl, is he?"

She accused him of dating her to help him get the job.

"How could I do that," he demanded, "when I won't tell anyone we even know each other?"

Uncertainty had hit her then, but before she could respond, he had walked away.

And he hadn't applied for the wrangler position, after all.

CARLY HURRIED ALONG the hallway, as if practically running toward the kitchen could help her escape her memories. With every step, she forced herself to slow down. By the time she reached the kitchen she had herself under control.

She crossed the room to the refrigerator. As usual, Anna had it stocked full of all kinds of goodies, including a plastic-covered crystal bowl filled with fruit and coconut and who knew what else. Her mouth watered at the sight of it. She had just finished rummaging through the crisper drawer when Anna spoke from behind her.

"Hands off that ambrosia, Carly. That's for dessert tonight."

"I wasn't even thinking about the ambrosia," she fibbed. She held up a ripe pear. "I'm going over to help Savannah, and this is my insurance against overeating when I get there. Those peach tarts of hers are just too tempting." She swung the refrigerator door closed and turned to find Anna eyeing her from head to toe.

"You could use a little temptation, if you ask me. Your last three visits, you've come back here thinner each time."

She stiffened. Anna's eagle eyes didn't miss much, which was partly the reason she had avoided coming home during those first few months of college. Even if no one else noticed, Anna would have picked up on the weight she had gained.

No longer dating Luke, cut off from her family by her own choice, afraid to confide in a roommate she really didn't know, she had turned to food after...

Food seemed to be the only comfort she had left. Food and sleep. But food didn't fill the empty place inside her, and sleep didn't take the pain away.

"I'm doing my best to put some meat on your bones again," Anna told her.

"I've got plenty of that, thank you very much."

"Then I should skip the biscuits and milk gravy I'm planning for supper tonight?"

"No, you should not. When I'm not home, I dream about your biscuits and gravy, Anna."

"Oh, please," the older woman scoffed, but her face softened with pleasure. Her greatest achievement in life was keeping the Baron kids fed, clothed and happy. "You always did have a good appetite, just as good as the boys."

"I weighed almost as much as they did, too, thanks to you."

"Nothing wrong with that."

"Ha." Carly took a deep breath and let it out again. "Anna, did Mom cook a lot?" At the housekeeper's frown, Carly rushed on, "I mean, we know I can't boil rice in a bag without having a fire extinguisher handy. But look at Savannah. She must've gotten her baking genes from somewhere."

"Some of that she learned in school."

"Well, maybe. But I took those classes, too."

"Those peach pies of hers that are so popular, she got that recipe from your mama."

"She did?"

"Sure." Anna gestured toward the ancient oak table she insisted on keeping as her work counter, despite its nicked and knife-scarred surface. "Don't you remember all the desserts your mama fed you when the other kids were off to school? Cakes and cookies and those peach pies? She liked to try things out first, before she served them to the family, and at that age, you wouldn't eat much else but sweets."

Slumping against the refrigerator, Carly stared at the table. Distant memories seemed to stir in her mind. Her mom with her sweater sleeves pushed up past her elbows to keep them free of flour... A frilly white apron with red strawberries for pockets... "Cakes and cookies... and milk in my plastic tumbler with the cowgirls on it."

Anna nodded. "That very one."

Carly smiled, both from the surprising comfort of the tiny sliver of newfound memory and to hide the stabbing pain that followed. "Yes, I guess I do remember some things."

The good things. The happy things. But she couldn't recall a single memory that would tell her why their mom had abandoned them. And at the rate Travis was progressing with his search, it looked as though none of them might ever know the truth.

Not meeting Anna's eyes, Carly polished the pear on her sleeve. "Guess I'd better be heading over to the Peach Pit."

"And I've got work to do upstairs."

After Anna had left the kitchen, Carly stared into space for a long moment. Then, sighing, she crossed the room to the back door.

Before she could reach for the knob, the door flew open. She jumped back to avoid being hit.

Jet barreled through the opening, almost colliding with her. She welcomed the sight of him, knowing he would distract her from thoughts that could rapidly turn into a case of the blues. "Hey! Easy, bro! What's your hurry?"

"Sorry about that. No hurry at all." He grimaced. "I'm responding to a summons from the old man."

"I just left him in the den."

"Yeah." He crossed his arms and leaned against the door frame, blocking her way.

It didn't surprise her that he wanted to linger out here in the kitchen. For a long time now, he and Brock hadn't been seeing eye to eye about Jet's role in the family oil business.

She had been there, had fought Brock's determination, too, and had the scars to prove it. If not for the all-out war he had waged to get her to take a job at Baron Energies right after high school, she might not have rebelled.

She might never have dated Luke.

Oh, no. Not going there again. She had control. "What happened to you yesterday? You left me hanging—and let Twister kick my butt."

"I got tied up at one of the oil fields."

"Oh, my. The boy actually works for a living. Who'd have believed it?"

"Very funny. Where are you headed off to?"

"Just out to the Peach Pit."

"Is that so?" He cocked his head, eyebrows raised, radiating disbelief.

She looked at him in surprise. "Would I have any reason to lie about where I'm going?"

"I never would have thought so. Then again, I never would have imagined you'd be walking home from our ranch manager's house. After dark, no less."

She felt her cheeks warm and hoped Jet couldn't notice any telltale sign in her face. "You saw me?"

"Wrong answer," he said. "The Carly comeback should have been, 'What's it to you, little brother?'" He grinned. "Something's up. Have you been a bad girl?"

Her mind flew to Monday night and Luke's house, when she stood so close to him with her shirt half off and his big, warm hand stroking her bare skin. A pleasurable shiver ran through her.

"Ah-ha." His brows rose again. "Maybe I'll have to have a talk with the old man about you."

"Jethro Horatio Baron." The sound of his hated full name made him grimace. "You say one word about… about anything to do with me, and I'll make sure Daddy knows just how eager you are for a management position."

He gave an exaggerated shudder of his own. "Okay, I give in. I'll keep my trap shut. But Jacob saw you, too."

She groaned.

Great. Savannah had told her their eldest stepbrother and Luke had been good friends ever since the two of them met at a rodeo a few years ago. Jacob could never keep from telling his best buddy the news about seeing her.

But why did she need to worry? Luke didn't have anything to tell Jacob, except the truth.

"Kim ditched me Monday night at the Longhorn." She raised her jaw. "Luke gave me a ride home. There was no point in making him drive a few hundred extra yards, so of course, I got out at his house. Then I walked home. That's all."

Jet laughed and tapped her nose with his fingertip. "That, my dear sister, is a perfect example of what you always warned us *not* to do. And I quote, 'When something goes wrong around here and Daddy calls for us one by one, don't rat anyone out. And don't *ever* volunteer information.' Unquote. Ring a bell?"

Of course it did. Experience had taught her at a young age to come up with those cautions, since she was often the first one summoned into the den.

She sighed. No matter what Jet said about keeping quiet, of all her siblings he was most likely to run off at the mouth. Desperate for some damage control, she rolled her eyes and shook her head. "Don't be ridiculous. I don't care *who* saw me. And I wasn't volunteering anything, just trying to outtalk *you* for a change." She pushed past him through the doorway and went down the front porch steps.

"Ha," he called from behind her. "If even I can tell you're hiding something, then good luck with Savannah. She'll see through you in a New York minute."

Cringing, she jogged toward the truck. Other than Anna, her second-oldest sister was about the only person she could safely talk to around here.

Yet, even with Savannah, she had too many subjects she couldn't mention.

"ANOTHER GOOD AFTERNOON'S WORK," Savannah said. "This is getting to be a habit."

"A good one," Carly assured her. "I'm glad for the distraction." Her sister couldn't possibly know the depth of her gratitude.

Savannah and her assistant, Gina, had been in and out of the workroom all afternoon. Every interruption dragged Carly away from thoughts of Luke and of the disaster that would have come from giving in to his request for one simple, so-called harmless, little kiss.

"I think I'm going to have to put you on the payroll," Savannah said.

She smiled. "You can't afford me."

"Probably not. At least, not yet. But…" Savannah winced. "I do have another favor to ask."

"More volunteer work?"

"You guessed it. Travis and I have decided where we're going for our postponed honeymoon. California wine country. We'll visit a few wineries, do some wine tasting and tour a handful of local farms. I'm hoping to get ideas for the store. So it's a business-with-pleasure trip."

"Sounds great. When are you leaving?"

"Well…we're hoping for this weekend, if we can get the reservations." Savannah sighed. "I know it's short notice for you—"

"It's perfect."

"Actually, it's not the best time for me to leave. But Travis and I are excited about the trip." Blushing, Savannah continued, "It would be good to have family overseeing things. Plus, the guys are working full-time out in the orchard right now, which means Gina would have to handle the store single-handed. You wouldn't need to come in all—"

"Savannah. Don't worry about it. After the day I had with Daddy, trust me, I'm ready for a break."

"Thanks." Savannah gave a sigh of relief. "I'll look into the reservations as soon we close the store tonight."

"And then just go and enjoy. With heavy emphasis on the pleasure part of the trip, I hope!"

Savannah turned even pinker, but grinned. She tapped the pastry box she had left on the worktable. "Speaking of pleasure…Luke stops in on Fridays to pick up a pie to take home."

"Considering it's only Wednesday, I hope you don't plan to stand here with that box, waiting for him." Carly eyed Savannah, who smiled innocently back at her. "But how nice for him. I'm sure he enjoys your pies, the way everyone else does."

Savannah laughed. "That's not what I meant, and you know it. I've been meaning to talk to you about him ever since the barbecue last week."

Now it was Carly's turn to flush.

Quiet, observant Savannah had always noticed more than any of the others in the family, and certainly more than Jet. Her raised brows proved she had caught the reaction. Her small smile indicated she planned to make the most of it. "I noticed the two of you seemed to get along…quite well."

"And that's not *quite* the kind of phrase you normally use, sister dear." Savannah was fishing for info, and Carly wasn't taking the bait. "I try to be nice to all the wranglers."

"Luke's not a wrangler or even just a manager. He's a lot more than that."

"Yeah, I know," she said grimly. "He's Daddy's right-hand man."

"Well, yes. With all the boys either tied up at the oil fields or running off to rodeo every chance they get, I think Daddy puts a lot on Luke. He places a lot of trust in him, too." Savannah smiled. "And you know Anna. The minute he started working here, she took him under her wing. Plus, I'm sure I don't need to tell you how hard we all fell for Rosie."

Eyes stinging, Carly bent quickly to slide a flat packing box out from beneath the workbench.

"But," Savannah continued, "what I meant was, Luke's practically family."

"No, he's not," Carly shot back. That was all she would need, to have him automatically considered part of the Baron brood. For her to be faced with more opportunities to think about and talk about and run into him.

"I don't see how you can make a fair assessment about it," Savannah said in a level tone. She leaned back against the opposite counter. "You haven't been around the ranch much since he started working here. You remember he'd lost his wife just a short time before that, don't you? That's why he quit the rodeo and took the manager position in the first place."

Carly fumbled with the box, attempting to assemble it. "Yes, you told me."

"He fits in well. And I think he appreciates being around people who care for his baby as much as they do for him."

As Carly yanked a strip of tape from the roll, she imagined a heart-sized bandage being ripped from her chest. The wound beneath it still hadn't healed. And she still didn't want to talk about Luke.

"Sorry," she muttered. "You're right. I wasn't being fair. But it's just..." She turned to face Savannah. "Everything's changed around here. You're married. Lizzie's being superwoman at the office, as usual, and now she's married and..."

"And pregnant. I can't believe it, either. What you mean is, we're all growing up."

"Yeah. And I think... I wonder..." Carly swallowed hard. "Mom's not here to see any of this." Or to know everything her children had gone through over the years.

"I wonder, too, Carly."

"Travis isn't any closer to finding her, is he?"

"Not yet," Savannah admitted. "But maybe every false lead is taking us closer to a good one."

"Or maybe the leads are drying up and we'll never know."

"We might have to face that, too. But Travis hasn't given up yet."

At her sister's stricken expression, Carly winced. Jet wasn't the only Baron with a big mouth. She moved across the room to give Savannah a hug. "Sorry, again. I wasn't blaming him or meaning to push. You two have lived with this longer than I have. And I…" She paced the length of the room and back again. "I know you don't plan to tell the family about your search, but I already know about it. And I want in. I want to do whatever I can to help you and Travis find Mom."

"I'm not sure you or I can do anything more than what he's done already. But you *are* in. As far as I'm concerned, you have been since I first told you about the search. But…Carly, are you okay?"

"I'm fine." She shrugged, struggling to think what to say. "There's just so much I want to tell her. To ask her. How could she not want to be a part of our lives? To know how we all turned out? How could she have just walked away from us?"

"I don't know. I wish I had answers." Savannah sighed. "Travis had me talk with Lizzie, even though I didn't tell her we planned to start a search. She didn't have any clues about where Mom could have gone. As for your questions…they're the kind Lizzie might able to help with. She was older, she might remember more. You should talk with her, too."

Her sister meant well with the obvious suggestion, but Lizzie was the last person Carly could go to. Not with the rest of the questions she had to ask. Questions she couldn't voice, even to Savannah.

Once Lizzie had passed her first trimester without

any further health problems, they had all sighed in relief. Still, Carly knew all too well that things could happen in the long weeks until Lizzie's due date. She kept her worries to herself and focused on happiness for Lizzie and Chris and their baby.

Away from the family, on her own, she had also cried a few frustrated tears over her struggle to deal with the pregnancy. She couldn't be more overjoyed for Lizzie, but the knowledge of her sister's baby filled her with regret. The sight of any pregnant woman flooded her with memories. With longing. With guilt.

Four years had gone by between the time their mom had given birth to Jet and then left them all. *Why* had she walked out? Did she have lingering issues from her final pregnancy? Had she suffered from postpartum depression...the way Carly had? Had her mom dealt with that depression for years afterward...the way she had?

How could she go down that road with Lizzie or Savannah? Neither of them had ever known she'd been pregnant. But with questions like those, they would wonder, suspect, might even ask her outright. They would want answers she didn't want to give.

The front door of the store opened. "A customer," Savannah murmured. "And Gina's gone for the day." She left the room.

Sighing, Carly reached for the carton and the tape dispenser.

As far as the family was concerned, her goal in coming back home again was to help everyone out. She didn't care what that meant—including pushing papers and a wheelchair for Brock or boxing up preserves for Savannah. She would do anything to keep herself busy, her mind filled, her memories at bay. Anything to save herself from drowning in the sorrows of her past.

But the Roughneck hadn't provided the escape she so desperately needed. It had only made her face her current reality. Dealing with the constant reminder of Lizzie's baby…and being forced to face Luke…

Nothing could have hurt her more than a reunion with him. Or so she'd thought—until she had seen the photos of him with his child.

A child, like her own, that she had never held, never touched. Never met.

Chapter Eight

"No rest for the weary, buddy?"

Luke sat at his desk in the office shoehorned into one corner of the barn. At the familiar voice, he looked up. Jacob Baron stood leaning against the door frame. "Jacob. When did you get back?"

"Yesterday."

"Carrying anything?"

"Another buckle, what else? You didn't expect me to come home empty-handed, did you?" Jacob gestured at the desk. "Looks like you've got your hands full, too."

"Same as always." The manager position had him spending almost as much time shuffling papers as working with his wranglers on the ranch. Considering he did most of the paperwork in his own comfortable living room while watching Rosie play with her toys a few feet from him, he wouldn't have traded the job for anything.

Yet, Monday night, he'd come much too close to throwing all his good fortune away.

"Haven't seen you around the arena much lately," Jacob said.

"I've been too busy to ride for pleasure." Luke looked at the order forms spread across the desk in front of him. "But that's going to change. In the near future, I'll be spending plenty of time out there."

In the past couple of days, Brock had asked more than once if he'd worked with Carly. Luke had come to the conclusion that he had no way out of the situation. Refusing would cost him this job and his chances of getting another one.

Like it or not, he was going to follow the boss's orders and give Carly Baron the tips that could help make her a champion bull rider.

What she did with the info was up to her.

How things went between them from now on was up to him.

He damned well wasn't going to come on to her the way he had Monday night. And yet, all week long, the memory of her with her shirt half off and her mouth close kept making it impossible for him to stay focused.

He shoved the order forms into a pile and clamped his jaw shut, knowing he couldn't say any of this to Jacob.

Friendship was one thing, family another. If he had a sister, he'd probably deck any man who walked around fantasizing over her. But no sisters for him. No brothers, either. He did have a daughter, though....

Lord help any guy Rosie brought home.

"It'll be good to see you out at the arena again. But what's got you thinking about more than the job all of a sudden?" Jacob asked. "Or should I say *who?*"

Luke tensed. "What are you talking about?"

"Your little tryst with my sister the other night, for one thing."

Damn. What the hell had Carly told her family?

"'Tryst?'" he repeated, stalling for time, straining to get his reactions under control. "I didn't think you even knew that word, buddy. Is that what she called it?"

"She who?" Jacob grinned.

Luke gathered up his paperwork and shoved the file

under his arm. "Carly, of course. Unless you're accusing me of putting the moves on a married woman."

"I wouldn't know what she called it, since Jet and I only saw her from a distance, walking home from your place. We were on the way out of here, and then I left town. I haven't seen her yet to ask her any specifics about it."

"No need to. I'll tell you. There was no tryst. I gave her a ride home."

"That's it? That's what she told Jet."

Relief shot through him. He rounded the desk. "Out of the way. I'm headed home."

Jacob followed him from the barn. "I'm disappointed in you, man. Carly's a good-looking woman."

Luke gaped at him. "She's also your sister. And you're...promoting the idea of me going out with her?"

"You could do worse." Jacob laughed. "Although, she'd run you ragged in no time. That girl doesn't give in on anything. What she *will* give you is a right hook, instead of listening to reason." He rubbed his jaw. "I speak from experience."

"Long-ago experience, I'd bet. She's got to have grown up some since then." Luke heard the echo of the words he'd said to her only last week, after he had walked out of this barn and nearly tripped over his own boots when he saw her sitting in the truck just a few hundred yards away.

By now, I would have thought you'd grown up some.

Judging by what he'd seen the other night, in some ways, she sure as hell had.

He forced his attention back to the other man, who stood there blathering.

"Well, yeah," Jacob was saying, "she's settled down

some since then. But she'll always have that wild streak in her."

Irritation flashed through Luke.

Did Jacob and the rest of the family really believe that about Carly?

Did that explain why she'd always tried so hard to put on the wild-girl act whenever he was around?

THE PEACH PIT looked to be doing a booming business, judging by the number of vehicles littering the area around the small building. As he entered the main room, Luke couldn't help grinning. Savannah had gotten herself into a sweet little deal here—much to Brock's surprise.

When they had talked yesterday, Jacob told him she and her new husband were leaving today for a couple of weeks, finally taking their honeymoon. Her assistant, Gina, smiled at him from behind the front counter, where she stood boxing up some tarts. "Luke," she said, tilting her head, "your pie's all ready for you in the workroom."

Nodding his thanks, he crossed to the far side of the room.

He stopped in once a week to pick up one of the Peach Pit's specialties—and one of Rosie's favorite desserts. She had been cutting new teeth for a while now, and a few mouthfuls of soft, cold peaches would be both a treat and a way to help soothe her. At least, for a few minutes. After that, he'd resort to the refrigerated teething ring.

He stepped into the workroom and found a sight to soothe him, too.

Alan Jackson sang from a CD player on a shelf above one of the workbenches, and Carly accompanied him, oblivious to any footsteps and unaware that he stood watching.

He hadn't seen her in days now, not since the morning at the arena, when she'd raced off on Pal as though he'd set a couple of herd dogs after them. And before that, at his house, when he'd…acted like a real dog himself.

He'd need to behave a sight better than that if he planned to work with her. And he did. There was no avoiding it.

No avoiding his reaction to seeing her now, either.

She was hunkered down in front of the bench, tugging at a plastic-strapped pile of flattened cardboard boxes. The worn denim of her jeans pulled tight over her curves. A sweet treat better than peach pie any day, even Savannah's. His mouth watered. His hands itched. And before he could stop himself, he'd sauntered over to stand just behind her.

"Need help?"

She let out a little shriek and stood, nearly cracking her shoulder on the edge of the table on the way up. She slapped the off button on the CD player and glared at him. "For Pete's sake, Luke. What are you doing here?"

"Came to see you."

"Right. And Daddy's converting the practice arena into a baseball training camp."

He laughed, though the reminder of Brock Baron and the arena set him on edge. "What are you doing here?"

"Filling in for Savannah while she's on her honeymoon."

Something Jacob *hadn't* mentioned the last time they met. But as Jacob didn't live on the ranch, maybe he hadn't known about the working arrangements. "I'm surprised your daddy went along with that, since you're supposed to be here to nurse him back to health."

"Considering all the time I was spending with him, I needed a break for my mental health."

"How's the rest of you doing?"

She frowned. "What?"

"Your shoulder."

"Oh. It's…coming along." She shot a glance at the table across the room. "Speaking of coming along, I know you didn't come here to see me. I just remembered Gina said you were stopping in to pick up a pie."

"Can't I do both?" He smiled. "But first, I'll pick up those boxes." He slid the pack out from under the table. "Where do you want 'em?"

"Over there." She gestured toward the table opposite and mumbled, "Thanks."

"No problem." He slid the pack into its new location and cut the plastic tape with his pocketknife. "All ready to go." She was leaning against the other table. What would she do if he moved in and put his hands on the tabletop on either side of her?

Probably give him a taste of that right hook Jacob had talked about.

He stayed where he was. "The boys were telling me you got in some practice on Twister." Before she could say anything, he shrugged and continued, "I'll be happy to give you some advice."

"Thanks, but what makes you think I need any?"

"How many hours have you clocked on the back of a bull?" he returned.

"On live ones, not many."

"How many?"

She sighed. "All right. Just the time I've spent on Twister this week."

"Then how about we set up a meet out at the arena. Tomorrow, late afternoon suit you?"

"No, thanks." She crossed her arms and winced.

"It's not coming along that well, is it?" An unnecessary question. He couldn't help noticing that her shoulder was sore. As many times as the cowhands said Twister had tossed her, probably a good many other of her parts hurt, too. Parts he didn't need to be thinking about....

He sure didn't wish the pain on her. But at least the situation gave him an excuse, too. A reason to keep his distance.

"It's just a twinge," she said. "But between daddy duty and filling in here at the store, I haven't got a minute to spare."

That worked in his favor, too. "We'd better hold off, then." Why did the idea fill him with disappointment? "To tell you the truth, I'm not sure why you want to do something so dangerous as ride bulls, anyhow. Just because it's the craziest thing you can think of to rile your daddy?"

"Oh, I've come up with much wilder plans in my past," she assured him.

"I'll bet you have."

"Besides, I'm beyond that." She looked away.

"Then what's with the bull riding? Still looking to find out where you belong?"

Her gaze shot back to his. "I can't believe you remembered that."

"Some things, I don't forget."

Her shoulders slumped, and she sighed. "I don't know. Maybe it's like I once told you. I can't compete with either of my sisters. And I don't want to," she added quickly. "We're all different, I know that. But Lizzie's a natural-born executive and a mother hen besides. And Savannah's such a homebody, so quiet and laid-back, yet she's gotten exactly what she wanted out of life. They know where they belong. They always have. And I...I don't know. Maybe bull riding is something I could do well." She shrugged. "How did we get onto this topic, anyhow? You came in to pick up a pie."

"Yeah, but while I'm here…" He might've gotten off the hook for now about giving her bull-riding lessons. That didn't excuse him from other obligations. He stepped in closer, conscious of Gina and the customers in the outer room. Carly stiffened, raising her chin. Her blue eyes looked wary. "No need to get uptight. I just wanted to apologize for what happened at my house. And to tell you it won't happen again."

"That's good."

"Yeah." Wasn't it? Then why did her easy acceptance make him feel another shot of disappointment? His conscience knew the answer to that better than he did.

Because you want a second chance at what almost happened Monday night—you damned fool.

That couldn't be an option. He might not have to work with her, but she was still the boss's daughter. He had to get along with her. Somehow. "Listen, Carly. We already agreed we can't go back. But we never settled about going forward. Personally, I don't see a reason we can't be friends."

She looked at him as if he'd just made an indecent suggestion. *"Friends?"*

"Yeah. You know, folks who stop and chat awhile when they run into each other."

She stood silent.

He tried again. "Folks who smile at each other once in a while."

Her mouth flattened into a firm line.

"All right, then, folks who *pretend* to get along with each other until one of them calms down and they can manage the real thing."

Her chin raised another notch.

So did his temper. "And especially folks who don't get their damned backs up the minute things don't go their way."

"Down, boy. Your hackles are rising."

Smug and insulting, all at the same time.

His temper got ready to rip...then she smiled.

"Carly, I swear—" He didn't know what he wanted to say. He didn't know what to do. Until her eyes gleamed. The damned woman knew she'd reduced him to standing there babbling like a fool. And she liked the fact.

Carly and his conscience. Between the two of them, he didn't stand a chance.

So...what the hell...

The look in Luke's eyes gave Carly full warning. She needed to get the heck out of Dodge. Or least out into the store's main room, where she would find Gina. Customers. Safety.

But by the time she ran through the list of advantages to leaving, she was trapped—by her own inability to look away from Luke.

Things began to move in slow motion, yet so rapidly they stole her breath.

He reached up to touch her face, to brush his fingers across her cheek. His roughened fingertips made her skin tingle, just the way the ointment on her shoulder had felt the other night. Only instead of cool cream, his fingers were warm and firm, curving along the length of her jaw, catching her chin and tilting it upward.

He moved in closer, towering over her, his body nearly touching hers.

She swallowed hard and pressed her tongue to the back of her teeth, fighting not to lick her lips instinctively. Not to give him any encouragement. Not to play the tease.

As if he understood her struggle, he smiled. As if trying to coax her into the action, anyway, he ran his thumb across her bottom lip. And then, as if he couldn't stand to wait any longer, he leaned down and kissed her.

It was like the first time they'd kissed, all over again.

It was like nothing she'd ever experienced.

It was like blazing new territory.

It was like coming home.

It was crazy, it was wild.

And allowing it to happen was the dumbest thing she had ever done.

She should have run when she'd had the chance. Should have gone into the other room.

At least she knew better than to let this continue.

She put her hands flat against him, almost losing her determination when the warmth of his chest spread through her palms and fingers. She wanted to curl those fingers into the fabric of his clean white Western shirt and tug him toward her, to pull him closer for another kiss. The intensity of the longing left her reeling.

Somehow, she managed to push him away.

"So, what exactly would you call that?" she demanded, her voice raspy. "An olive branch? A peacekeeping effort? The modern-day equivalent of a handshake?"

"I'd call it a step or two over the line from *friendly,*" he admitted.

"And not too smart."

"Maybe not. But nice. Very nice." He gave her a crooked smile that made her reel just a little more. "And now it's out of the way."

"What is?"

"The worry over when it was going to happen."

"Oh, *brother.*" He was lucky she didn't deck him. The nerve of the man, kissing her to make a point.

"Carly?"

Thank heaven for assistants.

Gina stood in the workroom doorway, smiling at them. "It's time to close up shop. Did you two take care of business back here?"

So much for thankfulness.

She studied Gina's face but found no sign of a smirk.

Luke, on the other hand, stood grinning at her. Why not? He'd taken care of business, all right.

The business of making her look like a fool.

Whether or not Gina had seen anything she shouldn't have, Carly had done something she should never even have contemplated.

"We were chatting," he told Gina. "I hadn't gotten around to getting my pie."

"No problem. I still have to finish my prep for tomorrow." Gina left the room.

Luke picked up the pastry box Gina had set on the worktable just before his arrival. "Thanks for the pie. But it can't be as sweet as what I just tasted."

Her face flaming, Carly bit her tongue and hurried into the outer room. She moved behind the counter to ring up the sale.

"Umm…Carly," Gina said. "Savannah doesn't charge Luke or his mom."

"Really?" She raised her brows.

"Really," Luke said.

Carly crossed her arms and looked pointedly at the box in his hands. "That's no way to make a profit. From now on, Savannah ought to make you pay double."

Gina laughed.

"She's a tough one, isn't she?" He spoke to Savannah's assistant, but his eyes never left Carly's. "At least, she pretends to be."

"No pretending about it," she fibbed, looking back at him without blinking. She needed to make him believe the words. Had to make him think he hadn't rattled her.

Considering the kiss they had just shared, she felt more desperate than ever to cling to her wild-child reputation. At this point, it seemed like the only defense she had left against him.

Chapter Nine

Carly left her truck in the parking garage and made her way to the lobby of the adjacent downtown Dallas office building.

Earlier that morning, Brock had mentioned Julieta planned to come back to the ranch to pick up some paperwork she needed from him. Instead, Carly had jumped at the opportunity to hand deliver the file. Normally, she would grab whatever chance she could to get *out* of the city—Dallas, Houston, any big city—but today, she would have done anything to get relief from the constant tension she felt at the Roughneck.

The teenage rebellion leading her to school in Houston had turned into the first step in her search to find where she might truly belong. That plan had backfired. Big-time. Her heart wasn't in Houston. She wasn't meant to be a city girl, though she managed to act like one.

And wasn't that her specialty—putting on an act?

As she waited for the elevator that would sweep her up to the corporate headquarters of Baron Energies, she attempted to figure out just how her return to the ranch she loved had gone so wrong.

She stayed with Brock for hours every day, teasing him out of his crankiness and catering to his every whim. Well…until she couldn't take it anymore. Then, she would insist on a break and head over to the Peach Pit. For a week now, she had filled in for her sister.

Before the newlyweds had departed for California, she had managed, casually, to gain another vital piece of information from Savannah about Luke's habit on Fridays. When he stopped in at the Peach Pit to pick up a pie, he never arrived until he was officially "off the clock"—though, of course, technically, he was never off duty. His job as ranch manager kept him on call 24/7.

Carly had thought the inside info would keep her path from crossing with his. She would just make sure to stay well away from the store at that time on that day.

Yet, in the week since Luke had come to pick up his pie…and had kissed her…he'd managed to catch her there every single evening.

Savannah couldn't have deliberately misled her about his schedule.

As Carly stepped into the elevator, a memory hit. She groaned, recalling her sister's comment about how well she and Luke seemed to get along. Had Savannah fibbed about Luke's habits to lure her into a sense of security? Had she wanted Carly to show up at the store, where she would be a sitting duck whenever Luke happened by?

Or…

Was Savannah telling the truth? And had Luke only taken to stopping in so often now because he knew he'd find her there?

A rush of pleasure shot through her at the thought. Ruthlessly, she squashed it. For days now, she'd battled another sensation, one that didn't please her at all—the certainty that she couldn't make a move on the ranch without fear of running into him.

The penned-in feeling had her primed to scream. Every memory of their kiss left her shaken.

Any way she looked at it, this had been one heck of a week.

She rode the elevators up to the office and stepped into the sleek, chrome-and-glass reception area.

Lizzie stood near the front desk, looking trim and professional in her maternity wear, a dark-blue suit with an unstructured jacket and a soft, white blouse. The clothing didn't call attention to her pregnancy, but didn't attempt to hide it, either.

Beside Lizzie stood a tall woman with long blond hair who also looked trim and professional in her *non*-maternity-wear suit.

"Carly!" Lizzie looked surprised but thrilled to see her. "What brings you here?"

"Courier duty." She held up the envelope she had brought from the Roughneck. "For Julieta."

"I didn't know you were delivering the file, but that's great, thanks." Lizzie looked at the other woman. "J.C., this is my sister Carly Baron. Carly, meet J. C. Marks. J.C.'s applying for an engineer position with us."

"Nice to meet you," J.C. said to Carly. She turned to Lizzie and shook hands. "Thanks so much for your time this morning."

"Yours, too," Lizzie said. "We'll be in touch once we've finished the first round of interviews."

The woman rang for the elevator. After leaving the file for the receptionist to give to Julieta, Lizzie took Carly by the arm. "I'm not letting you get away. Come on, let's go back to my office."

They went down the wide hallway toward the large room Lizzie occupied. She asked her assistant to hold all calls, then escorted Carly into the office and closed the door behind them.

Lizzie took a seat on a small leather couch and

FREE Merchandise is 'in the Cards' for you!

Dear Reader,

We're giving away FREE MERCHANDISE!

Seriously, we'd like to reward you for reading this novel by giving you **FREE MERCHANDISE** worth over $20. And no purchase is necessary!

You see the Jack of Hearts sticker above? Paste that sticker in the box on the Free Merchandise Voucher inside. Return the Voucher promptly...and we'll send you valuable Free Merchandise!

Thanks again for reading one of our novels—and enjoy your Free Merchandise with our compliments!

Pam Powers

Pam Powers

P.S. Look inside to see what Free Merchandise is **"in the cards"** for you!

W

e'd like to send you two free books like the one you are enjoying now. Your two books have a combined price of over $10, but they are yours to keep absolutely FREE! We'll even send you 2 wonderful surprise gifts. You can't lose!

REMEMBER: Your Free Merchandise, consisting of **2 Free Books** and **2 Free Gifts**, is worth over $20.00! No purchase is necessary, so please send for your Free Merchandise today.

Get TWO FREE GIFTS!

We'll also send you two wonderful FREE GIFTS (worth about $10), in addition to your 2 Free books!

Visit us at:
www.ReaderService.com

YOUR FREE MERCHANDISE INCLUDES...

2 FREE Books **AND** 2 FREE Mystery Gifts

FREE MERCHANDISE VOUCHER

2 FREE BOOKS and 2 FREE GIFTS

Please send my Free Merchandise, consisting of
2 Free Books and **2 Free Mystery Gifts**.
I understand that I am under no obligation to buy
anything, as explained on the back of this card.

154/354 HDL GEYY

Please Print

FIRST NAME

LAST NAME

ADDRESS

APT.#   CITY

STATE/PROV.   ZIP/POSTAL CODE

NO PURCHASE NECESSARY!

AR-714-FM13

propped her legs up on it with a sigh. "I gave J.C. a tour of the office, and my feet are saying that wasn't such a good idea."

"You ought to give up those heels for a while."

"Or buy bigger shoes." Lizzie smiled. "I need to keep looking as professional as I can. When you're surrounded by the old boy's network, it's a double disadvantage to be a pregnant female."

"You don't have anything to worry about. Daddy wouldn't have put you in charge while he was gone if he didn't trust you could do the job."

"Thanks for the vote of confidence, sweetie." Lizzie's eyes gleamed. "Have a seat. It's been a while since you've dropped by the office. And now that you're here, can I talk you into applying for a position with the Baron family?"

Carly froze as an image flashed into her mind: Luke, in threadbare jeans but a brand-new shirt, showing up at the Roughneck to apply for a wrangler's position.

"Carly?"

Seeing Lizzie eyeing her, she forced a smile. "You know better. I wouldn't fit in here at all."

"You could, you know," Lizzie said softly. "Daddy would have a job created for you."

"That's just what I don't want. I want to succeed on my own." To be the best at *something*. And, as Luke had remembered after all these years, to find out where she belonged.

After finishing school in Houston, she had stayed on, gotten an apartment, tried one job and then another until landing the sales position she now held. A position she'd taken a leave of absence from for an unspecified length of time. None of this provided the solution she wanted. None of it satisfied her. Maybe nothing ever would.

Even the thrill of bull riding had already started to wane.

She took a seat on the chair nearest the couch. "Your situation is different, Lizzie. You're perfect for the company. You always have been. I'd be such an odd fit, Daddy would *have* to tailor-make a job for me, just to give me something to do."

Lizzie shifted on the couch, pulling the white blouse down over her rounded belly.

Carly linked her fingers together in her lap. "Enough about that idea. How's…how are you feeling?"

"Fine. Just tired. I'm not used to carrying all this extra weight."

"You're lucky you don't live at home anymore. Anna would be feeding you double portions of everything."

Lizzie laughed. "I know. She tries that whenever Chris and I are at the ranch for dinner."

"Well, regardless, you two ought to stop by again soon."

"Is Daddy driving you crazy? Or have you got someone else distracting you these days, too?"

Carly's fingers clamped together. "What are you talking about?"

"Savannah and I were catching up before she left—"

"Gossiping, you mean?"

"Let's say, having a sisterly chat." Lizzie laughed. "She seems to think you and Luke have hit it off. And after what I saw at the barbecue, I couldn't disagree."

"We didn't do anything." Carly's cheeks heated. "I mean, we didn't hit it off. I'm…friendly…with everyone on the ranch. You get along with all the company employees, don't you?"

"True." Lizzie smiled. "But getting to know Luke wouldn't be a bad thing. He's such a nice guy. And he's doing a fabulous job raising his daughter. It's not easy being a single parent."

"Yeah." Carly almost choked on the word. After a long silence, she said, "You'll be able to take good care of your baby, won't you?"

"Of course." Lizzie's forehead wrinkled in a frown.

"What would you have done if you and Chris hadn't decided to get married?"

Lizzie rested her hand on her stomach. "Brought up the baby on my own. Carly, what's wrong? For a while now, I've had the feeling there's something bothering you. Can we talk about it?"

At the concern in Lizzie's voice, guilt gnawed at her. Shifting the conversation to Lizzie had been a bad idea. A very bad idea. But she'd needed the diversion because she didn't want to talk about or think about or envision Luke.

And because she desperately wanted answers to questions that had shadowed her life for years.

She walked to the wall of windows and stood looking at Lizzie's view of the downtown Dallas skyline. "I've just been thinking a lot about what you said about Mom a couple of months ago. And what you didn't say. And I've been trying to put the pieces together. She had postpartum depression, didn't she?"

"I think so."

"And I didn't know."

"It makes sense that you wouldn't. You were so young when she left. I didn't know myself until I thought of some of the memories I had of her and did some reading on the subject."

"Are you worried you might have it, too, after the baby comes?"

"I'm not thinking that far ahead. But if I do suffer

from it, I won't keep it to myself. And," Lizzie added, "you and Chris and everyone will help me get through it."

She turned to face Lizzie. "Of course we will." She hesitated, then said, "I never told anyone, but when I was away at college my first year, I had an issue with depression."

"Carly." Lizzie began to lower her feet.

"No, stay there." She returned to her chair.

"Why didn't you ever tell me? Or Savannah?"

She shrugged. "I don't know. I wanted to tough it out myself, I guess. It's okay, I got through it. It's just that the experience, and then thinking about Mom…that makes me relate to her. Makes me want to talk to her and ask if that's why she left us."

Lizzie covered Carly's fingers with hers. "I wish we knew, too, sweetie. But after all these years, I'm not sure how much luck we'd have trying to track her down."

Not much.

She couldn't say that. She couldn't break Savannah's confidence.

"I tell myself," Lizzie added, "we all just need to keep looking forward."

Right.

First Luke. Now Lizzie. Both with the same thought. Yet she couldn't keep from focusing on the past.

Maybe because she was the only one to have a secret hidden there.

Which was where it would have to stay.

She couldn't share her history with Lizzie, now so happily pregnant. She couldn't talk to Savannah. She couldn't tell anyone in the family about the baby she had carried.

The baby she had lost.

She couldn't reveal her secret to anyone at all.

Not when she had never told Luke.

AFTER HIS SHOWER, Luke looked at his reflection in the bathroom mirror and took a deep breath. Time to go beard the lioness who'd made herself at home in his den. Otherwise known as his mother.

Trying to get away with something with Tammy around was always tough. Trying to get Rosie away from her was nigh-on impossible. But he'd give both his best shot.

He found Tammy on the floor in the living room, patiently taking one stuffed animal after another from Rosie and adding it to the growing pile beside her. He knew that game. As soon as Rosie had handed over the last stuffed toy, she would demand them all back again.

"Mom, I think I'll give you a break from animal grab and take this little girl off your hands for a while."

Tammy looked up, her head cocked and her eyes narrowed. "And just what are you up to?"

"Nothing." At the sound of his voice, Rosie had turned to reach up to him. Smiling, he lifted her into his arms. "Can't I go off with one of my best girls without the other one getting curious?"

Tammy laughed. "Curiosity has nothing to do with it. Confirming my suspicions, is more like it. Why would you need a two-year-old along just to pick up some dessert?"

He frowned. "Who said that's where I'm going?"

"Your truck's been spotted outside the Peach Pit more than once this week. I never knew you to have such a sweet tooth."

"Maybe I've had a hankering for a homemade pecan roll lately."

"Uh-huh. And that's not all, so I hear."

"What does that mean?"

"Carly Baron's working at the store while Savannah's away."

"Yeah, so?" Hands flat, fingers spread wide, Rosie smacked his cheeks. Knowing what she wanted, he took a deep breath and held it. She shrieked and smacked him again, and he directed his puff of breath toward her forehead, ruffling her blond curls. She giggled.

"So…why didn't you just come right out and tell me you wanted to go over there?"

He lowered himself onto a chair and set Rosie on his knee. She watched, waiting for him to puff up his cheeks so she could smack them again. He obliged. "Because," he said over his daughter's shrieks, "if I told you, you'd give me the third degree. The way you are now."

Her laughter mixed with Rosie's. "I haven't even begun yet, and you know it."

"Yeah." He gave her a rueful smile. Growing up without a dad had made him and his mom close. Had made him respect her for all she had accomplished on her own and made him love her for all she had sacrificed. But that didn't mean he liked sitting still for her questions.

He liked even less the idea that someone ran to her telling tales about him. Especially when they involved Brock Baron's little girl. "Where are you getting your info?"

"Anna's been keeping an eye on the store, since she knows Gina's working alone. She happened to mention seeing your truck. Anything wrong with that?"

That depended on where else the woman "happened to mention" her news. He'd heard nothing from any quarter. Until now.

"Does it need to be a big secret, Luke? If you want to see Carly, what's the harm?"

Besides the fact she was always going to be Brock Baron's little girl and he was always going to be the kid from the poor side of town?

He couldn't—wouldn't—say that. His mom had done so much for him, but he was beyond the stage where she could make things all better. Some things she couldn't control. Neither could he. He just had to live with them.

Like the days he had spent in school, dealing with some of his friends. The so-called friends who had turned traitor on him, accusing him of cheating his way to success, instead of accepting that he'd worked for it. And like the day that Carly had accused him of using her for the same reason.

He couldn't share that with his mother, either. He had never told her any of it. But there was one thing he could say now.

"I'm not seeing Carly, Mom. Not the way you mean."

"And what would be wrong with it, if you were?" She smiled and reached up to tug on Rosie's soft shoe. "This little one's getting to be a big girl. She needs a mama."

"She's got you."

"I'm Gramma, sweetheart, not Mommy. And you need someone, too."

He shook his head. "I'm fine."

"Are you? I've never said a word to you before this, and I wouldn't now, if I didn't know you were done grieving for Jodi. And it's been two years. There's no disloyalty to her if we all have to move on."

Rosie squirmed, and he stood. "This girl and I are moving on right now."

Tammy sighed. "I'm not pushing you, sweetheart. I just want you and Rosie to be happy. You know that."

"I do."

As he buckled Rosie into her carrier in the truck, he thought about his mother's final words.

She wouldn't push him.

Maybe he ought to be pushing himself.

He *had* come to terms with Jodi's death, had finally learned to accept it. Along the way, his life had fallen into a rhythm. A familiar pattern. Work and ranching and wranglers, home and Rosie and his mom.

He couldn't give all that up for just any relationship— especially not one that hadn't lasted the first time around.

Once a bull had thrown you, you were out of the running. Done.

If you were lucky, you walked away in one piece. But you'd always come back to try again.

If you knew what you wanted, that was. If you truly had your eye on the prize. If nothing could stop you from proving you were just as good as the next man...

Chapter Ten

A few minutes later, Luke pulled up in front of the Peach Pit.

The boss had been on his case again, and Luke had spent the past several days listening to Carly's half-hearted assurances that she would go to the arena with him. Soon.

Her excuses about needing to help out at the store made him back off, but they weren't going to satisfy Brock forever. He'd made it clear, much as he didn't want Carly riding bulls, he also didn't want her leaving the ranch without having gotten some instruction from Luke.

"Today, Rosie," he said as he parked the truck, "we're not taking empty promises for an answer." He unbuckled the restraint on her carrier in the backseat. "Either her shoulder hurts too much and needs some attention, or her shoulder's healed, and I need to follow through on the assignment the boss gave me. Right?"

"Da." She slammed her hand on the side of the carrier.

"Right."

He kissed her petal-soft cheek, then nuzzled it with his nose, knowing she would laugh. And she did. Life for Rosie Nobel was just one big bowl of cherries.

Or maybe peaches.

There was no way anyone could *not* love his baby girl.

Which was why it beat the hell out of him when, every time he mentioned her name, Carly changed the subject.

"We're not taking that today, either, are we, Rosie? Let's see her talk about something else when you're right there in front of her face."

And Rosie *would* be right in front of Carly. When he'd stopped in yesterday, Gina had told him she planned to take off the last couple of hours of her shift today. Carly would be working solo.

Deliberately, he had waited until the last few minutes before closing time to arrive at the store. Other than her truck, his was the only vehicle in the parking area.

He and Rosie found the main room empty. Carly must have stepped into the workroom or the kitchen. He took Rosie on a tour of the store, showing her the jars of peach preserves, the plastic-wrapped pecan candies and the glass-fronted display case filled with pastries and pies.

When she spotted the pies, she squealed and threw her hands above her head. *"Whoa, girl."* He managed to stop her just before she could slap her little fingerprints all over the spotless glass.

"I'll be right with you," Carly called from the kitchen. A moment later, she came into the room carrying a stack of pastry boxes. "Sorry, I didn't hear—" Frowning, she cut herself off and stared at him. "Luke."

Her reaction confirmed three things for him. She hadn't heard the door. She hadn't heard his voice clearly enough to recognize it. And she didn't like seeing Rosie in his arms.

She lifted the boxes to a high shelf, then took a stack of empty metal trays from beneath the counter. "I'm just wrapping things up for the night."

"Then you can wrap up one of these peach pies for me."

"Fine." She carried the trays into the kitchen.

Through the open doorway, he could see her set them on top of a tall floor cabinet. "Looks like the shoulder's doing pretty well," he called.

"Not well enough to handle Twister." She returned to the front of the store and took down a pastry box.

Her refusal to look his way riled him. He'd had enough of her acting as if he were the invisible man. *And* of her ignoring his daughter. "All right, then," he persisted, "if you're not ready for the back of a bull again, why don't we just take a couple of horses and go for a ride. Tomorrow. When you're off work. Rosie will be with my mom for a while."

"I don't—"

"Meanwhile, when you're done tonight, how about we sit and have a chat with Rosie?"

For a moment, her hands stilled halfway toward the peach pie on the top shelf. "I don't have that much time. I need to get back to the house."

Rosie looked on, fascinated, as Carly slid the pie from the display case. He smiled, feeling his jaw clench. She wouldn't have noticed his daughter's interest. She didn't bother to look up.

"This would be Rosie," he said. "I don't believe the two of you have met."

Slowly, Carly raised her head. Her eyes widened, and her face turned as white as the paper liners on the display case shelf.

Damn. What was it with her?

All right, any baby could be intimidating when you weren't used to being around kids. But there was something more to Carly's uneasiness than just being near his daughter. Her reaction tonight only confirmed his growing suspicions. Whatever was bothering her, it had something to do with kids....

Or was it *his* kid, specifically?

Maybe Carly's behavior had nothing to do with feeling intimated and uneasy at being around Rosie. Maybe she felt uncomfortable at the reminder he'd had a child with someone other than her.

The idea might make him rethink Carly's actions.

But it couldn't do anything to change their history.

"Well. And what do we have here?"

Luke didn't need to look to know who had spoken from behind him. He turned, anyway. Brock Baron stood leaning against the doorway, a pair of crutches braced beneath his arms.

"Daddy?" Carly said, her voice strained. "How did you get here?"

A moment ago, Luke had blamed the shock in her eyes and her suddenly pale face on his insistence that she look at Rosie. But obviously, he'd been wrong.

Her concern had come from seeing Brock.

"I drove him here," Anna said, appearing in the doorway behind the boss.

"You did?" Carly asked.

She sounded surprised. Maybe she thought she was the only good nursemaid around.

Brock moved forward and took a seat at a small table Savannah had set near the front window. It couldn't have been more than a couple yards from the parking area to that chair. But lines of fatigue in the man's face showed how much the short walk had cost him.

Still, when he saw Rosie, he managed a smile.

Carly hurried out from behind the counter. "What are you doing up on your feet? Do you want to set back all the progress you've made? And maybe add to the damage?"

"I tried to tell him," Anna said, "but he wouldn't listen."

"I know what I can and can't do," Brock said.

"And we'll see what the doctor has to say about that." Carly stood with her hands on her hips, glaring down at him.

The sparks in her eyes sent Luke's blood rushing down around his own hips. But her outright defiance of her daddy left his head spinning—and not in a good way. Nobody talked to Brock Baron like that and walked off without getting a strip torn from his or her hide.

Nobody witnessing it fared too well, either.

Anna could fend for herself. But he needed to get Rosie out of here. It was bad enough he slipped and used some questionable language around her once in a while. He didn't need her hearing worse from his irate boss.

He lifted the boxed pie from the counter. "Don't forget our ride tomorrow," he told Carly. "I'll see you at the barn once you close up the store. Anna. Brock." He nodded at them both.

After a quick stop while Brock chucked Rosie under the chin and Anna gave her curls a kiss, Luke took his little girl out of firing range.

BROCK STRIPPED OFF his shirt and watched his wife combing her hair at the dresser. When her eyes met his in the mirror, he said, "You know, you're one fine-looking woman."

"That's why you married me, isn't it?"

He smiled at the familiar joke and gave his usual response. "Looks and brains."

"You couldn't pass up that combination, could you?"

She smiled back at him, then set the comb down and turned to face him. "What's this I hear about you over-doing things today?"

He exhaled sharply. "That darned girl. She needs to keep her opinions to herself."

"Who? Carly? Not likely, when she's as outspoken as you are. But Carly didn't tell me what you've been up to. Anna did."

"And that woman had better remember who provides her with room and board and a steady income—or she'll find herself out of a job."

"You'd never fire Anna, and you know it." Julieta shook her head. "We all had better hope the doctor re-leases you to go back to *your* job soon. You're turning into a cranky old man."

"Old? Come over here, and we'll see about that."

She laughed. "Don't try to change the subject. I also heard about what Carly said to you. And she has a valid point. You don't want to cause any permanent damage by doing more than you should too soon."

He waved the comment away. "Did Anna tell you we found Luke sniffing around at the Peach Pit?"

"So?"

"While Carly was working. They're supposed to go for a ride tomorrow. A horseback ride, she said."

"Well, it's a step toward what you wanted, isn't it? Getting them together, so Luke can take her in hand and give her some advice on bull riding?"

"I don't want her on the back of a bull at all. But yes, if she's going to be stubborn enough to go through with her idea, I want Luke giving her some guidance. I didn't say anything about putting his hands on her."

She laughed, loud and long, until she had to wipe tears from her eyes. "Brock, if you could have seen your face just now." She came over to take a seat on the bed, close to where he sat in his wheelchair. She squeezed his arm. "You've got nothing to worry about there. Carly's a grown woman."

"Without much sense."

"She has plenty of good sense. You just don't want to see her as anything but your little girl. And what's the problem, anyhow? You trust Luke."

"I do."

"Well, then?"

"We'll wait and see."

She shook her head. "Oh, Brock."

"Don't 'oh, Brock,' me." He glared. "It doesn't matter how well you think you know a man. You can never tell what he'll do when he's given enough rope to hang himself."

A LONG RIDE in the northern acres left them at the supply cabin closest to the house, where they stopped to rest their horses.

While Luke checked the condition of the cabin, Carly climbed up to sit on the adjacent fence and enjoy watching the sun sink. Though they still had plenty of light left in the day, their ride home would have them headed east, away from the sunset.

They hadn't talked much at all since leaving the barn, but to her surprise, the quiet had been companionable.

She had felt reluctant about showing up to meet Luke.

At least she had good excuses to keep her from climbing onto the back of a bull again. She didn't want to think about him giving her riding tips and loathed the idea of him watching her struggle to manage a live bull. But even her loss of control in a situation like that wouldn't compare to how she felt at being with him.

She drained her water bottle and set it on the fence rail beside her. Finished his inspection, Luke crossed the space between them and stopped a few feet away.

She gripped the rail on either side of her. "This was a pleasure ride—or so I thought. And here you are working. Are you always so thorough when it comes to your job?"

"I try to be. With the job and everything else."

A shiver ran down her spine at the suggestive words. But, darn him, he simply looked back at her steadily, without a sign of teasing in his expression.

"You were that way with your job at the garage, too."

"I did try with that, too. No matter what anyone else thought."

"Why would anyone think something different?"

"Folks come up with crazy notions."

"About you? Straight-arrow Luke? I don't believe it. Notions like what?"

"Like I wasn't always such a straight arrow. They accused me of playing the advantages to get whatever I wanted."

She had once done that, too.

"At least," he continued, "that's what some folks said. But those days are over. So is this one, almost." He turned his head and squinted against the glare of the lowering sun. "We'd better head back soon, before we lose the light."

She nodded, accepting the change of subject. For now.

He smiled. "Did you enjoy the ride?"

"Yes, actually."

"You sound as if you didn't expect to."

"I didn't."

One look at his face at the Peach Pit last night had told her he wouldn't accept no for an answer about taking her out on horseback. Besides, he'd had her trapped. "I didn't want to go on this ride at all. You knew that. But you also knew I wouldn't give you the satisfaction of arguing, with Daddy and Anna standing right there."

He rested one hip against the fence, toasted her with his water bottle and grinned. "Thanks for giving me credit for that much, at least. How did it go after I left?"

"I'm still standing, aren't I?"

"Sitting, technically." He looked her over from head to toe. "You do that well. And you don't do badly on the back of a horse."

"Thanks for nothing."

He shrugged. "Hey, it *is* nothing compared to riding a bull. I gave you an easy out."

"*Easy?* You'd better not let Daredevil hear you say that."

He took a long swig from his bottle, throat muscles working hard. "You just had to choose the most cantankerous horse in the stable, didn't you?"

She smiled. He'd nearly had a conniption when she had led the stallion, already saddled, out of the barn.

His mouth curved in a half smile. "Daredevil might be bullheaded—like some people I know—but he's still horseflesh. And my offer to help with the bull riding tips still stands."

Dang. After her sessions with Twister, she wasn't a hundred percent sure she even wanted to ride a live bull again.

And, after the way everything had ended between them, she couldn't believe Luke Nobel still wanted to help her. Worse, she couldn't believe what she still wanted from him—and it involved a heck of a lot more than tips on how to ride a bull.

An offer like this one, from a champion rider...

Turning him down would make her seem as wild and crazy as her family had always thought.

On the other hand, accepting his offer, agreeing to get close to him, would prove her just plain crazy.

He eyed her for a moment then snapped, "You've just dropped onto the back of a bull. What's the most important thing you need to do?"

"Now, *that's* easy. Find your seat."

He shook his head. "Try again."

"Get your balance."

"Nope. What body part do you rely on most?"

"Your dominant hand."

"And you want to ride bulls?" he scoffed. "Wrong on all counts."

"All right, then. This." She braced her hands on either side of her, just inches below her belt. "Right here. It's all in the hip action."

Smiling, he leaned forward, till their lips almost met. His eyes seemed to glow. "Well, now," he breathed, "you are…absolutely…*wrong.*"

"What?" She recoiled in astonishment and almost toppled off the fence.

He grabbed her around the waist to brace her, then took her hands and rested them on her thighs. He pressed his hands flat atop hers, his warm palms covering her fingers. A prickly sensation ran through her, like sparks from an electrified fence.

"Not the hips, Carly. A little lower. Here."

He rested his hands on her knees. Then he slid his palms upward again. He had hooked his strong thumbs against her inner thighs, exerting more pressure the higher his hands climbed. A bolt of heat slammed through her middle.

When he'd reached the midpoint of her thighs, he

stood still. "This is what'll keep you hanging on tight. What you use to grip that bull."

With him standing so close and her body heat spiked so high, she wanted him to be teasing her, playing with her. She wanted him to have another meaning hidden beneath his words.

But he stared at her without even the hint of a sparkle in his eyes.

Dammit.

She stared back silently at all that had so briefly been hers. The dark blond hair, the color of sand, that she'd always loved to run her fingers through. The sturdy jaw with its deceptively soft-looking stubble that had once buffed her teenage cheeks to a rosy glow. And the eyes... those honey-brown eyes... Like none she'd ever seen before.

They were warm and caring and trusting. And, oh, how she wished she could tell him the truth. But she didn't dare. If he knew what she had been keeping from him, he would never trust her. He would never even come this close to her again.

"Thanks for the tip of the day." Her voice sounded too loud in the quiet, too shaky for her liking. "I think we'd better head home."

Now he would say something suggestive and mean it. Now he would make his move.

And she would have to gather the emotional strength to push him away.

Instead, he simply stepped back.

She jumped down from the fence and started toward Daredevil on legs twice as shaky as her voice had been.

LUKE HAD NO IDEA what the hell happened.

Once minute, Carly was walking away from him to

mount Daredevil, and the next she was flying through the air.

He ran toward her, too late to stop the memories of Jodi's accident from battering his brain. Too late to save Carly from her fall.

He saw her hit the ground, head and shoulder first. He saw her tumble and land spread-eagled flat on her back.

He didn't see her move.

"Carly!"

Daredevil pawed the dirt inches from her head.

Luke grabbed the reins, looped them around the fence and made sure his own mount stood quietly at a distance.

Heart in his throat, he dropped to his knees beside Carly.

Her eyes didn't open. And still she didn't move.

"Carly."

He took a deep breath and told himself she'd be all right. This wasn't going to end like Jodi's fall. She wouldn't be paralyzed. She wasn't going to die.

Her breathing was even, her pulse steady.

As he took another calming breath of his own, her eyelids fluttered. He reached for her hand.

She opened her eyes and looked up at him, her brow wrinkled in a frown. "What's—?"

She shifted her free arm, but he stilled her movement. "Just lie there a minute."

For once, she didn't raise an argument, which worried him more than anything else.

She worried him. Ever since he'd seen her on the ranch again, he had known something wasn't right. Something was bothering her. Something she had no intention of telling him.

Once, she would have confided in him. Not anymore.

And now this.

He never should have suggested the ride. *He* should have argued with her the minute she had insisted on taking the stallion.

"What happened when you mounted Daredevil?" he asked.

"I—I don't know. I don't remember."

That wasn't good. "Don't move," he warned her again. "Just tell me what hurts."

"My shoulder." Her grin looked forced. "But that hurt, anyway."

"So much for it coming along. What else?"

"Nothing that I can feel."

That might not be good, either. "Okay, we'll go slow." He took her through turning her head, then moving one arm or leg at a time, making sure she had feeling in every limb but no pain. Finally, he eased her to a seated position. "How's that?"

"Fine. I don't hurt at all."

"You will later. But at least it seems as though you didn't break or sprain anything."

"Good." She laughed. "I can just imagine getting stuck in a cast and in a wheelchair, right alongside Daddy."

He managed a smile. "If I were you, I wouldn't laugh just yet. I have a strong suspicion once he hears about this, he'll get you tied down one way or another."

"Then he can't hear about it."

He stared at her. "Are you crazy? That would be more than my life is worth, not to tell him about this."

"Then they'll all be sure I'm as irresponsible as they've always believed."

"Because you had an accident? I don't think so."

Her eyes narrowed. "You're not telling him anything."

"Wrong. The second I get you home, I'm telling every

damned person in that ranch house. You had a bad fall. And you don't remember it happening."

"I *do* remember it. I just don't know why Daredevil threw me."

"That's a huge distinction, isn't it?" he said dryly. "What it boils down to is, you don't recall what happened. On top of that, you hit your head. And you were out for more than a few seconds."

"I'm fine."

"So you say. I'm telling your family—"

"I'll tell them."

"Right."

"You don't trust me?"

"This is too important to play games with, Carly. I've been through this before. I know what can happen."

She shifted, and he helped her to stand. She seemed steady enough on her feet.

"We'll take a slow ride back," he told her. "You'll let me know if anything starts to hurt. You take Chestnut. I've got Daredevil."

"I should ride Daredevil. You know what they say when you fall off a horse. You need to get right back in the saddle."

"Keep pushing that idea, and you won't be in a saddle at all. You'll be wearing out boot leather."

She made a face but, without another word, headed toward Chestnut.

She wouldn't stay so quiet once she heard what else he had to say.

He'd best get her back to the barn before he dropped that bombshell.

Chapter Eleven

After their ride back home, Luke wanted her to stay at his house for the evening. So he could keep his eye on her for a while, he said. Carly had argued until her tongue felt ready to fall out, but there was no budging him.

"I don't want to scare you," he said finally, "but you could have a concussion. Or worse."

The look in his eyes when he'd said those words made her swallow her protests and give in. He was concerned about her. He was also thinking of Jodi. There was no way she could—or would—fight that terrible memory.

Just as there was no way she could fight all the wonderful memories he must have of his wife.

Sighing, she shifted on the couch.

Luke left her there and disappeared down the hallway. A short while later, she had heard the shower running. After her long day, she could have used a shower, too. Wild-child Carly would have marched right down that hallway and joined him.

She stayed on the couch and tried to distract herself with a magazine from the coffee table, then mindless flips through the television channels.

He had come back into the living room with his hair still damp and his keys in his hand, on his way to pick up Rosie from his mom's house.

Again, she had opted to stay on the couch. Not out of cowardice—or so she told herself. Their ride had made her feel closer to him, and being alone in the house, just the two of them, made her want to get even closer. She'd needed the distance and had insisted she would be fine on her own.

Her solitude ended when his front door opened and he entered, carrying his daughter.

"Say hi to Carly, Rosie," Luke encouraged.

"Da-da."

He laughed. "We're still working on 'hello.' Mom fed her already. She said Rosie's on the cranky side, though, from the teething. Aren't you, baby?" He kissed her forehead and set her on the floor beside the huge pile of stuffed animals. "Were you okay while I went to get Rosie?"

"Fine." Except for the aches and pains, and the slight headache that had developed while he'd been gone.

"Keep an eye on Rosie for a minute. I'll go and get dinner out of the truck."

She curled up on the couch, wrapping her arms around her folded legs and looked across the room. The little girl gave her a grin then flopped back into the pile of stuffed toys.

Carly's throat tightened.

Rosie held a stuffed animal out to her.

Her heart sank. When she had agreed to stay for a while with Luke, she hadn't thought about having to deal with his daughter. And when he brought the child home, she had hoped he would put Rosie right to bed.

Instead, Rosie sat there staring at her, her arms fully extended, holding the stuffed elephant by his floppy ears and slamming its head against the floor, over and over again.

With the way her own head was ringing, Carly felt compassion for the poor toy. She just didn't want to get near Rosie.

The front door swung open again. Luke entered carrying a plastic bag in one hand and a pizza box in the other. He set the box on the coffee table. "She wants you to take the elephant," he explained. "Then she'll want you to take everything else."

She nodded and twined her fingers together in her lap.

He frowned. "You sure you're all right?"

"Yeah. I…uh…don't have much experience with kids."

"What about Alex?"

Alex was her youngest stepbrother, Julieta's five-year-old son. "I don't see him very often."

"Well, you'll need to get in practice, with Lizzie's baby on the way." He grinned. "Lucky for you, Rosie will break you in."

No, Rosie would *break* her—if Luke didn't do it first. Already, with those two short sentences, he had managed to put another crack in her fragile emotions.

When Luke returned to the living room with a couple of plates and cups and a bottle of pop, he seemed surprised to see her still sitting on the couch.

Rosie began to babble, her voice rising higher and higher. Would tears follow? Screams? A full-out tantrum?

Carly didn't know. She didn't know anything about kids and didn't want to learn. Not now. Not here.

But Luke stood staring at her.

Rosie's voice rose another notch.

"She won't give up," Luke told her. "That's typical, from what I've seen. Especially with girls." He raised his eyebrows, as if making sure she got the message.

"Very funny."

With a sigh, she lowered herself to the floor beside the couch and crawled the few feet to Rosie.

Screeching, the little girl slapped the battered elephant into Carly's lap.

CARLY ATE A couple of slices of the pizza. When Luke had finished polishing off the rest, he moved to sit on the floor beside Rosie. They went through the same routine Carly had done earlier, with Rosie passing every stuffed animal to him and then taking them all back. After that, they moved on to some complicated game that involved building blocks, a plastic fire engine and three dolls.

Hugging her knees, Carly sat watching them, noticing how unselfconsciously Luke played the games with his daughter, how intently he focused on her, as if he and Rosie were the only ones in the room. How often his eyes lit when he smiled at her.

Carly's eyes stung with tears, blurring her vision. She imagined him with another child, one with hair a lighter shade of blond, maybe, and blue eyes instead of brown.

"Hey," Luke said softly.

She froze, her fingertips touching her cheek.

"Tired?" he asked.

He must not have noticed her tears. She nodded and, relieved, brushed away the remaining traces.

"You and Rosie," he said with a smile.

She glanced past him. To her surprise, she saw his daughter lay half asleep against the pile of stuffed animals. She had been so caught up in thoughts of Luke, she'd lost track of time. How long had he been watching her before he'd spoken, bringing her back to reality? Maybe she didn't want to know.

He scooped Rosie up from the floor, murmuring, "Bedtime for you, my little girl."

Lizzie was right. Luke was a good daddy—and the confirmation only made her feel worse.

This was turning out to be the worst night of her life.

As soon as he came back, she was out of there. She would go home and, just as they had agreed, would tell Anna about her fall. Better for her to be at the ranch house and under Anna's care than in this small house with Luke just a few yards away.

He came back carrying the familiar jar of ointment and a towel. "Rosie's all tucked in. And now, time to take care of you. Where does it hurt?"

Reaching desperately for her only defense, she forced a grin. "What would you do if I said 'all over'?"

He grinned back at her. "Get ready to have a good time." He set everything on the coffee table and took a seat on the couch beside her. "But seriously, where?"

"My neck and shoulder," she admitted.

"Nowhere else?"

"Well…maybe both shoulders." Everywhere else, she could reach herself.

"Let's go, then. I'll close my eyes till you're ready."

She pulled her shirt over her head but kept her arms in the sleeves, leaving herself more covered than if she wore a bathing suit. Turning her back to him, she drew her legs up and wrapped her arms around her knees. "Okay. I'm ready."

In the quiet of the living room, sounds seemed magnified. She heard him exhale a heavy breath. Heard the rattle of the lid as he opened the jar of ointment, the clatter as the lid landed on the coffee table.

Then his hand was on her shoulder, spreading the pungent ointment that managed to feel cold initially and then warm as he worked it into her skin. His other hand rested on her neck. For a moment, she froze, aware of how vulnerable her position might be…with another man. Not with Luke.

She trusted him.

His hands stilled.

She lowered her chin to her knees.

After a moment, he continued, caressing her shoulders with both hands, then using his strong thumbs to knead the muscles in her neck. She thought of those hands on her thighs as she'd sat on the fence earlier that day. Her cheeks burning, she rested her face against her knees and gave thanks that she sat facing away from him.

What seemed like only a moment later, she heard the jar thudding onto the coffee table.

"Let me go wash up."

By the time he returned, she had her T-shirt on again and was sitting with her back braced against the arm of the couch. He took a seat beside her.

"Just checked on Rosie," he said. "She woke up some when I put her to bed, but she's out like a light now."

"Mmm-hmm." Carly didn't know what else to say.

Her mind might be empty, but her heart felt full, as always weighed down by sorrow and now even heavier with regret.

This evening with Luke and his little girl had just about done her in. Again, she admitted Lizzie was right. Luke was a good daddy. And more.

Watching him with Rosie…hearing how he teased his mom…seeing his gentleness with her after the fall from Daredevil…all this made her admit what she had always known.

Luke Nobel was a good man.

"What did you mean this afternoon, when you said people believed you played advantages?"

He shrugged. "Let's just say folks thought things came my way too easily."

"How could they? You worked so hard. Just because they had money and you didn't—"

"I'm not talking about that," he said. "It had nothing to do with money. It wasn't wealthy folks putting me down. It was the kids I went to school with. Kids who didn't have two nickels to rub together most days, either. The guys I called my friends."

"That's awful. Why would they treat you like that?"

His jaw tightened for a moment, then he said, "I worked damned hard for everything I got. They wouldn't admit that because they weren't willing to do the same. They wouldn't fight like I did for the things I wanted. Good grades. The job at the garage. A scholarship."

"You'd gotten a scholarship?" She couldn't keep the surprise from her voice.

"Shocking, huh? Hard to believe about someone like me?"

"Of course not. I'm just surprised because you never told me about it. You said you'd never gone to college."

"I hadn't, at the time I met you."

"But what about the scholarship? Why didn't you use it?"

"My mom lost her job at the refinery and couldn't find work. I added on to my hours at the garage for a while, and that didn't leave me time for school."

She frowned. "But for the ranch manager position, Daddy…"

"Requires someone with a degree." He nodded. "Once I started doing well in rodeo, I quit the job. I had enough to take care of Mom and the time to go to school. By the time I retired from rodeo, I also had my degree."

With all the tabs she had kept on him, she'd never heard about that. What else didn't she know about him?

They sat in silence for a moment. She shifted, resting her hand on the cushion at the back of the couch.

"What's the matter? All these true confessions making you uncomfortable?"

She forced a laugh. "Not a chance. Since you insist on keeping an eye on me here for a while, I'm just settling in. You couldn't make me uncomfortable if you tried."

"Wish you could say the same about Rosie."

She froze.

"Why are you so uptight with her?"

"I—I told you, I'm just not good around kids."

"You know what they say, practice makes perfect."

"And obviously, you've had a lot of practice."

He smiled. "Are you saying I'm perfect?"

Perfect for me. Once. A long time ago.

He reached up and covered her hand with his.

She jumped.

He nodded, as if confirming a thought. "You're uptight around me, too. You're sure I'm not making you uncomfortable?" He'd kept his tone level, with no hint of playfulness or teasing.

"All right—yes, I'm uncomfortable," she admitted. "But not from being with you. From…a lot of reasons. From wishing things were different. Wishing I could take back what I'd said to you."

"About me using you to get a job on the ranch."

She nodded. "I flew off the handle. For a minute, I honestly thought that's why you wanted to go out with me. It felt like you'd betrayed me, and when you wouldn't answer, I thought it was true. I wasn't thinking straight. And you didn't deserve what I said."

"I can't blame you for that, because I let my pride get in the way of telling you the truth."

"The truth?"

"Yeah. Applying here at the Roughneck had nothing to do with using you. You didn't want your daddy knowing we were seeing each other, and just as I told you, I didn't plan on mentioning your name. To anyone. I only wanted that wrangler job because it would put me closer to you."

She swallowed hard. "Oh, Luke. Why didn't you tell me?"

"Why didn't you trust me?" he asked softly. "That's what I felt then. I'd worked so hard for *everything* I'd ever gotten. My friends didn't believe that. And that day, neither did you."

He reached up and brushed her hair away from her face, then traced a path with his fingertip from her temple, down her cheek, along her jaw.

When she sighed, he wrapped his arm around her and pulled her close. She leaned against him, resting her forehead against his shirt, suddenly unable to face him. She had been so cruel in the way she had accused him back then. She hadn't been much nicer to him in these past few days. Another thing he didn't deserve. "I'm sorry, Luke."

He touched her cheek, slipped his hand beneath her chin to tilt her head up and looked into her eyes.

She tried for a smile. It felt tentative. So did she— until he tightened his free arm around her, holding her even closer, and lowered his mouth to hers.

She kissed him back with all the enthusiasm of the teenager who had once loved him, all the longing of the woman who had since lost him, all the confused, crazy, mixed-up emotions of the wild child she had to pretend to be.

She had never loved Luke more, never wanted him more....

But one apology couldn't erase the past.

One confession couldn't solve everything, couldn't sweep away her problems, couldn't keep her from understanding she didn't deserve another chance for happiness with him.

She had realized that already, earlier this evening, hadn't she? Watching him with Rosie had told her the truth. Luke loved his child...and would have loved *their* child, too.

She couldn't risk getting this close to him, close enough to make her want to open her heart.

His mouth still on hers, she shifted in his arms, ending their kiss and laughing as if she didn't have a care in the world. Pretending that her heart wasn't breaking.

"Wow." She gasped. "That made my head spin."

"Yeah, mine, too."

"No," she said. "Not like this." She put a hand to her forehead and winced, not from pain but from guilt at the lie she had to tell. "That fall might've done more damage than I thought. Maybe you were right, after all, and I've got a concussion."

Her statement had the not-so-desired but necessary effect of putting an end to any more kisses—and to anything else he might have had in mind.

It almost resulted in a trip to the hospital or, at the least, a call to the Baron family doctor.

She had to backtrack immediately, making light of what she'd said without admitting she had fibbed. At the same time, she pretended to let slip she'd had second thoughts about a make-out session on the couch.

"There's no sense in looking for anything more than this," she said honestly. "I'm only here on the ranch for a little while. And then it's back to Houston again."

"I know."

"Which means it's better not to start anything between us."

His eyes narrowed as he gazed at her.

He didn't like that decision.

Neither did she.

At least she had sounded convincing enough to get him to back off about calling in a doctor. He insisted upon checking her pupils with a penlight, made her stand up and walk a straight line and asked her a series of simple questions.

Finally, he appeared satisfied she was okay for the short walk to the ranch house. "Anna's got to wake you periodically through the night to check for signs of concussion. I told you, you need to make sure of that, or you're spending the night right here."

"And I already told you, I'll arrange it."

Those ideas didn't please her, either. Having Anna hovering over her versus Luke and his couch. She had opted for the lesser of two evils.

Now, idiotically, she wished she had made the more dangerous choice.

Chapter Twelve

In the week after the horseback ride, Carly spent every waking moment either with Brock or immersed in work at the Peach Pit. She desperately needed to distract herself from thoughts of Luke and the feelings of hopelessness and guilt that seemed to increase every time she went near him.

Her time at the store, especially, left her open to the chance of running into him. She counteracted that by staying away just before suppertime, when he had most often stopped in, and by making sure they were in sight of Gina or a customer whenever he was near.

The day after their ride, he had managed to corner her to ask quietly how she was feeling—and to verify that she'd had Anna check on her through the night. She had rolled her eyes, trying to minimize the importance of her fall, but admitted she had done as promised.

Since then, he had come in daily to pick up a pecan roll or some peach tarts and his regular Friday-night pie. If only Gina hadn't told her about not charging the darned man, she could have added a nice chunk of change to the store's profits while Savannah was gone.

Today, she had arrived at the Peach Pit to find the usual Saturday crowd in the store. Finally, after an hour, she and Gina had a chance to exchange a few words.

"We received a delivery this morning," Gina told her, "a supply order Savannah put in before she left. I was busy when the deliveryman showed up, and I had him set the boxes on the worktable in the back. I'm afraid I haven't had a chance to touch them since."

"No problem. When it slows down out here, I'll unpack and check the contents, then you can help me stash them away, since you'll know better where everything should go."

Gina nodded. "It's all nonperishable items, and fortunately Savannah has plenty of extra storage room upstairs. We're going to need it."

In the early afternoon, Carly went into the back room and got to work. With only half the boxes unpacked, she had to agree with Gina about the space upstairs. There wasn't enough room here or in the kitchen to store the surplus.

Cross-checking the supplies against the packing list and Savannah's order took her a good part of the afternoon. Maybe that was because her mind frequently strayed from the job.

With the honeymooners due home in a couple of days, she would soon have no reason to spend as much time at the store. Still, she looked forward to their return, when Travis would continue his search for Delia Baron. With luck, he would have more success this time around.

Sighing, she set the paperwork aside and eyed the worktable, so full of the items she had unpacked that she had nowhere to work. Until Gina could join her and show her the extra storage space, she would refill the packing boxes temporarily....

Her hands stilled on an empty carton.

Thoughts of boxes, temporarily stored, triggered a memory.

Getting ready to leave for college. Packing up her personal belongings.

Those she didn't plan to take with her had gone into separate boxes, which she had taken up to the attic of the ranch house, away from prying eyes. Not that she thought her family would go through her bedroom while she was gone. But Brock might have had an overflow of guests and needed to offer her room to someone. Anna might have wanted to do some fall cleaning.

Later, once Brock had married Julieta and her son had grown into a mischievous little boy, Carly had been just as glad to have her personal items stored in the attic, in boxes that were taped shut and had her name scrawled on them.

Now, instead of wanting to work at the Peach Pit until the last customer had been waited on and the door was locked for the night, she couldn't wait to leave and get back to the ranch house.

Inside those boxes in the attic, hidden among half-forgotten childhood and teenaged treasures, she might discover something of real value.

She might find something that would lead them to her mom.

SHAKING HIS HEAD, Luke dropped the file folder of invoices on Brock's desk in the den. In the past few days the boss had turned into a *micro*micromanager. Worse, he'd hounded Luke about the bull-riding lessons.

Luke never lied, and Carly's story about being too busy at the store had worn too thin for his liking. Savannah and Travis were due back in a couple of days, at which point her excuse would wear out altogether.

Since her fall from Daredevil, he'd had plenty of opportunities to see her at work at the Peach Pit. She moved effortlessly and without a single grimace. As far as he could see, she was ready to ride.

But he'd had his doubts all along about what she had said to her daddy. Something told him she had no true desire to ride bulls, period.

Early on in their relationship, he'd seen the vulnerability in Carly. Yet he had never fallen for her wild-girl act, no matter how he played along. Her interest in bull riding was as false as that act of hers had always been, a mask she put on only because she had something to hide from everyone. Including him.

He wondered what it was she couldn't bring herself to tell him.

But what did it matter? She had made the obvious even more plain—there was no sense in their starting anything between them. As if he would, anyhow.

He had a daughter she wouldn't go near and plans for more kids in his future. A future he wouldn't be sharing with Carly.

He wished now he'd kept his mouth shut with her about his past. What had made him tell her about the scholarship, he didn't know. Maybe the need to make her see he wasn't the opportunistic bastard she'd always thought he was.

And that didn't matter anymore, either.

He turned to leave the den.

A heavy thud sounded overhead, followed by a series of crashes. Followed by dead silence.

He hurried out into the hallway. "Brock? Anna? *Carly?*"

No answer.

They would be the only ones home at this hour of the day, and he already knew they weren't downstairs. He had checked the ground floor when he arrived.

He headed for the stairs, calling their names again. More silence.

At the far end of the hall on the second floor, a door stood ajar. As he approached the opening, the attic floorboards groaned. Someone was up there, and he doubted it would be Brock on his crutches. "Anna?"

He took the stairs three at a time.

In the center of the huge room, Carly knelt on the floor, surrounded by open packing boxes marked with her name.

"What the hell happened?" he demanded.

She flinched and looked up at him, wide-eyed, as if she hadn't heard him until just now. "Luke?"

"What's going on? What was all that noise?"

She gestured behind her. "I knocked over a few boxes of Anna's extra baking pans, I think." She stared down at the cartons around her.

He frowned. Every day this week, he'd swung by the Peach Pit after work, yet he'd never managed to get her alone. That was deliberate on her part, he felt sure. She wanted to avoid seeing him at all.

If so, she was much too laid-back about seeing him now. And she hadn't heard him calling her name. Whatever those cartons contained, they had caught and held her attention.

On the floor beside her rested a short stack of beige envelopes tied with a pink ribbon. He had never seen the ribbon before, but he'd put money down for a bet on those envelopes.

He eased onto a plastic-shrouded rocking chair and linked his fingers together in front of him. "Looks like you saved my letters."

She glanced down at the pile and flushed. "Guess so. I'd forgotten they were in here."

The ribbon was still tied tight, which meant she hadn't come up here just to read the few sweet nothings he'd sent her. So, this wasn't a trip down memory lane. Or was it? "What are you doing up here?"

"Looking through these boxes."

He laughed softly. "Well, right. I can see that for myself."

She sat back on her heels and ran a hand through her hair. "I came up here to try to find a piece of my past."

But not the part that included him.

She took a deep breath and held it, as if she didn't want to say anything more. A second later she let the breath out in a whoosh and looked at him, her eyes shining. "*Luke.* I think I might have a way to find my mom."

For a moment, he sat speechless. He'd never forgotten the story she had once told him of how her mother had walked out on them all. Just up and left one day and never came back. Carly had been five years old when that happened, and she never seemed to have gotten over it. "You're kidding. A link to your mom, after all these years?"

She nodded. "Savannah and Travis have been looking for her, though Savannah doesn't want the family to know. When I finally remembered about these boxes up here, I thought maybe I could find something to help. And look."

Any reluctance she might have had to be with him had now disappeared in her excitement to show him what she'd discovered. She pushed aside a box and held out a stack of drawings, curled at the edges from having been rolled up and tied with another ribbon.

"I drew these when I was a kid. Who knows why the heck I ever saved them. But look at this."

She handed him one of the drawings. When he unfurled it and held the edges flat against his knees, she came to his side and pointed to the stick figures lined up on the page. The first figure had a cloud of yellow hair and a couple of red splotches in the vicinity of her stomach. "That's Mom in her apron with the strawberries on the pockets."

"I thought they were bloodstains."

She shoved his arm. "What do you expect, a masterpiece? I was five years old when I drew this." She pointed to the next two figures, one with a round body and a beehive of brown hair, the other half-size and wearing a wide grin. "That's me and Anna."

"Looks just like you." He pointed to the last stick figure with its tall, emaciated body and an unruly mass of red curls. "And who's this?"

"That's…" She faltered. "I don't know. She was at the house a lot, always in the kitchen with me and Mom and Anna. Now that I've seen these drawings again, I remember her face clearly. I just can't recall her name. But," she added, sounding more confident, "Anna will know."

The excitement in her face was at odds with the worried look in her eyes. Both told him how much she was depending on the older woman to have answers. What if Anna didn't know the woman's name? What if she didn't recall anything about the woman at all?

At five years old, Carly had been hurt beyond belief. At eighteen, she'd still been vulnerable over her loss. What would it do to her, all these years later, if this clue she believed she had found came to a dead end?

Or worse?

"I hope you find out who this is," he began cautiously. "But after so many years—"

"I know. You don't need to say it. There's a chance Anna won't remember. Or even if she does know the woman, we might not be able to track her down. We've already hit those kinds of roadblocks," she said bitterly.

"Carly." He rested his hand lightly on her wrist. "Family's important. I get that, especially not having much of my own. I don't know what I'd do without Rosie or Mom." Her arm jerked beneath his hand. "But you have lots of family. And you're important to every one of them."

"I know that. They're just as important to me."

"They love you."

"I know that, too. And I love them." She frowned. "What are you trying to say?"

"Just because your mom left, it doesn't mean she didn't care about you. Or that she didn't love you."

She looked away.

He moved his hand from her wrist and curled his fingers around hers.

She looked back at him, her eyes bright. "Those are things I don't know for sure. And I won't, until I find out her reason for leaving."

He sighed. "Then I hope you're right and Anna's got the name you're looking for."

Good thing the drive from the Peach Pit to the ranch house was short, with no traffic, and nearly a straight line, because Carly covered the few miles in a brain fog. She had so much on her mind, she could barely focus.

But she was conscious enough to see the rider on the chestnut horse cantering parallel to the road. She pulled to the side, opened the door of the truck so she could stand on the running board and waved to get Luke's attention. He waved his Stetson and headed the horse her way.

Her heart suddenly pounding, she closed the door

and waited for him to approach the truck. She'd waited just as impatiently at the Peach Pit tonight, but he hadn't come into the store. So ironic, after all the time she had spent trying to avoid being alone with him this week.

He dismounted and stood beside the driver's door. "What's up?"

"I talked to Anna last night. She remembered the woman's name."

His eyes lit. She had the window fully open and her hand on the door frame. He rested his hand on hers and gave her fingers a squeeze. Her heart tripped, but she told herself not to get excited. He'd held her hand in the attic yesterday, too. Then, he'd felt sorry for her. Now, he only wanted to share her excitement.

"That's great," he said. "Have you found her?"

She shook her head. "No, I tried. But I didn't get far. Travis has the resources. I'll talk to him when they get back."

"This sounds like cause for a celebration. Have dinner with me tomorrow?"

She hesitated, wanting to say yes, wanting to be with him again, yet knowing how foolish it would be to accept. Besides, she couldn't go out then, anyway. "I can't. We're having a family dinner to welcome Savannah and Travis back."

"Monday, then."

Hadn't she told him they needed to keep the past in the past? That she would be headed back to Houston soon?

Those were the reasons she had to turn him down.

Yet, she wanted to accept his invitation. Though they couldn't have time alone, she could have that one last chance to cherish being with him. And to say goodbye.

A friendly goodbye she hoped might help to make up for their angry parting years ago.

Her heart ached, much worse than the way her body had after a go-around with Twister.

"All right," she agreed. "But let me bring dinner this time. And…and something for Rosie."

He smiled slowly, then shook his head. "Thanks for the offer, but no takeout, no kids. I'm talking dinner out, adults only. I'm taking you out on the town."

CARLY'S SUNDAY MORNING passed in a blur. Half of her felt excited that Savannah and Travis would be home soon and she would be able to tell them what she had discovered. Half of her felt filled with dread over her upcoming date with Luke.

She wasn't sure she would be able to eat a bite of Anna's pork roast and homemade applesauce. Then again, with all her brothers here for dinner, she'd probably be lucky to get more than a few bites to begin with.

Lizzie and Chris had already arrived and were in the living room with Brock, Julieta and Alex. Jacob had greeted everyone and then disappeared, most likely on a visit to Luke's.

For a moment, she worried that Luke might mention something he shouldn't, might forget she had told him the family didn't know anything about their search. Well, sooner or later, once they found Delia, everyone would have to know.

She was setting out glasses on the kitchen counter when her stepbrother Daniel came in to get a drink. Though he was Jacob's brother and the two looked a lot alike, their personalities couldn't have been more different. Daniel was quieter, with a tendency to think too much and too deeply if left on his own for long and a wry sense of humor she appreciated. She smiled and handed him a tea glass. "Have we heard from Jet?" she asked.

He nodded. "A text. He's on the way."

"Late as usual. That's Jet. Then it looks like you're drafted to help me and Anna. When you've gotten your drink, could you carry this tray of glasses into the dining room?"

"Sounds like work."

She laughed. "So was making that pitcher of homemade lemonade you're headed for. And cooking the dinner you're going to be eating soon."

"I get your point."

The sound of loud voices and laughter floated down the hall from the front entryway. "The newlyweds must have arrived."

"Must have." Daniel hoisted the tray. "Nobody would get that excited over Jet showing up."

"That's terrible, Daniel." Laughing, she followed him down the hall. "Don't you dare say that to him."

By the time everyone had greeted Savannah and Travis, and they had all taken seats around the table, Jet had joined them. He immediately stood at the table and proposed a toast to the newlyweds. Everyone clinked glasses and wished them well.

"And," Jet said, "I propose another toast. To the lucky grooms, Chris and Travis, with a big thank-you for helping to meet the Baron family wedding quota for the year."

"I second that," Jacob said.

"Yeah," Daniel agreed. "It lets the rest of us off the hook."

"Oh, I don't know," Lizzie said. "I think we could stand to have another engagement around here, at least, don't you, Savannah?"

Savannah nodded. "I sure do."

Carly froze. Lizzie and Savannah both looked at her.

The entire family looked at her, except Julieta's young son. For one long, horrified moment, she thought everyone but five-year-old Alex must know she was…talking with Luke.

Then even Alex startled her by announcing, "Carly has to have her turn next."

She took a sip of sweet tea to ease her tight throat before asking, "Why is that, Alex?"

"Because," he said, "Mom says girls go first."

"Ah. Well." She smiled at Lizzie and Savannah. "Don't worry. If I'm ever able to whittle down my long list of admirers to a manageable number, y'all will be the first to know."

Chapter Thirteen

With dinner over and most of the family gone home, Carly claimed she needed to bring Savannah up to date on the store. It gave her an excuse to follow Savannah and Travis to the Peach Pit.

They were both ecstatic over the new lead she had discovered.

"I wasn't able to find out much from Anna besides the woman's name, Genevieve Caron. Anna has no idea where she lives. I tried searching but didn't get anywhere."

"Don't worry about it." Travis didn't sound at all discouraged. "Internet searches can turn up a lot of info, but it's not always the most reliable or comprehensive. And the woman might have gotten married or divorced or had another reason for changing her name. I'll start digging first thing tomorrow." He kissed Savannah's temple. "I'm heading upstairs so you two can talk shop."

Savannah smiled and touched his hand.

Carly took a deep breath. The teasing aside, dinner had been fun, though seeing Savannah and Travis and Lizzie and Chris all so happy…so content…so *newlywed* had almost done her in. Like another toss from Twister. Another kick to her heart.

If only things had worked out with Luke the way they

should have, she would have been the old married lady of the family by now.

One with a family of her own.

That thought was too devastating to dwell on. She pushed it aside, said goodbye to Travis and set about filling Savannah in on what had gone on while she was gone. They had kept in touch sporadically via email, but Carly hadn't wanted to bother her with every little detail.

When they had finished their business, Savannah cleared the table in the kitchen and made a pot of tea. She also set out a plate of peach tarts.

"Mmm." Carly reached for one. "Just what I need on top of Anna's blueberry crumble. I'll be having to go home sooner than expected. I didn't bring any sweats with me, and that's about all I'll fit into, if I keep this up."

"Do you have to go home?"

She laughed. "I was teasing. If necessary, I'll just keep the button on my jeans open."

"No, seriously. I mean, do you have to go home at all?"

Carly set the tart down on her dessert plate. She'd had a sudden vision of returning to Houston to hand in her notice. "You'd better watch throwing questions like that around. I might get you to put me to work—permanently. But of course, you'd have to give me more than just a paycheck. I wouldn't settle for less than a partnership."

To her surprise, Savannah said eagerly, "Carly! That's just what I've been wishing you would do."

And to her surprise, Carly couldn't think of anything she would enjoy more. Or of anything that would be so impossible.

To live here on this ranch…to be within a stone's throw of Luke's house…to run the risk of seeing him every day…

She couldn't do it.

Thoughts of their dinner out had already given her more than she could handle. But she still wanted that time alone to say her goodbyes.

"I've got a job in Houston," she reminded Savannah. "But if I did come back, I'd consider the Peach Pit. Better than you and Lizzie ganging up on me again and trying to convince me to apply at Baron Energies."

Savannah blinked. "That's the last thing I'd try to do. But when did we ever gang up on you?"

She rolled her eyes. "Uh…like a couple of hours ago, at the dinner table."

"Oh, that."

"Yes, *that.*"

Savannah grinned over her teacup. "How's everything going with Luke, by the way?"

"It's…" Carly looked down at her plate and shook her head. "I don't know what it is. We're getting together tomorrow night. I thought it was just going to be a casual thing and I'd bring takeout over to his house, but he says he's taking me out on the town and I don't know what to do. I don't know what to wear. I don't—"

"Whoa, girl. Take a deep breath and settle down."

She laughed shakily. "Sorry. I guess it just hit me that we're talking tomorrow night and I…"

"You're in a panic, that's what you are." Savannah's laugh wasn't shaky at all. "I can't believe this. Do we need another shopping trip, or what?" She shook her head. "What happened to the woman who'd instructed me about how to handle a night with a man—emphasis on the *night?*"

"Best advice you ever got, wasn't it?"

Savannah giggled. "You're darned right. And now I'm giving it back to you."

"I don't think Luke and I will be getting to the night-gown stage." A sudden vision of them together, with no clothes between them at all, almost had her choking on a mouthful of tea.

What the heck was Savannah serving her, anyway, that was causing these crazy hallucinations?

"You never know what can happen," Savannah told her. "But that doesn't matter. A night on the town requires the proper outfit. In other words, sister—*dress to impress.* And when it's all over, be sure and thank me for the reminders."

LUKE TOOK A slug of sweet tea and forced it down his tight throat. Dinner had gone reasonably well—no, dinner had been great. But he'd had a helluva time keeping his mind on his meal.

Carly had shown up at his house in an outfit guaranteed to distract him. Black high heels added three inches to her height and made her legs look impossibly long. A short black skirt hugged her hips and butt. A gauzy white shirt let him see right through to the tank-top-like thing beneath, a scrap of shiny white fabric hanging from nearly nonexistent shoulder straps. None of this did a damned thing to help him focus on the plate in front of him.

And if all that wasn't enough to keep his attention riveted, the long strand of pink pearls that kept dipping into the valley between her breasts was giving him a permanent hard-on.

"I…um…I'll be going back home again soon."

She sounded nervous. Why, he didn't know—unless his face had given away his thoughts. He sure hoped not. But he did his best to breathe deeply and forget about how she had dressed…for him.

"You said that the other day, about going home. Is Brock past the stage of needing a nurse?"

"He's coming along."

"I guess you've got folks missing you."

"A few. And a job waiting."

"What was it you said you did?"

"I'm in outside sales for a Western wear company."

He swallowed a grin. The way she was dressed, she ought to be a buyer for women's wear. Men all across the country would thank her. "You enjoy the work?"

She shrugged. "I like dealing with customers. The rest of the job is okay. But I've got to pay the bills. And my student loans."

He frowned. "You took out loans? Your daddy wouldn't cover all your school expenses?"

"He didn't cover any of them. What I couldn't get through scholarships, I paid for myself."

He bit back a surprised curse. He'd never do that to Rosie. "The sexist SOB. I know he helped Jacob."

"Jet and Daniel, too. Oh, Daddy wanted to take care of everything—once he got over being peeved I didn't want to live at home and commute to school in Dallas. But I wouldn't let him pay for my school. I wanted to do it myself."

"There's that independent streak again."

"Looking back, I see now it might've been just plain pigheadedness." She laughed and toyed with her string of pearls.

He reached for the check the waitress had left on the table. "Dessert? More coffee? Anything else?"

"No, I'm good."

More than good.

He dropped a few bills on the table with the check. "Let's go, then."

He held her chair. Once she'd stood, he reached for her hand. For a moment, her fingers seemed to stiffen. Then she curled them around his.

They walked through the lamp-lit restaurant and out to the sidewalk. They had arrived for a late dinner, and he had found a parking space for his truck in a far corner of the lot. He took his time walking, not wanting to let her go.

Not wanting her to leave him.

The thought hit him like a punch to the gut, and he involuntarily tightened his grip on her hand. To his surprise, she returned the pressure of his fingers.

At the truck, still reluctant to release her, he unlocked the passenger door with one hand.

Her shirt shimmered in the lights ringing the parking lot. Her eyes shone. After they had eaten, she had slicked on some pink lipstick, and that had a shine to it, too.

Before he could think twice, he leaned down and kissed her. The lipstick tasted sweet, like bubblegum. Or maybe like just pure Carly.

He wrapped his free arm around her shoulder and urged her close—dangerously close to his champion belt buckle and the hardness beneath his jeans. But he didn't hold back. She had to know she turned him on. She had to know how much he wanted her.

And it seemed she did. Her hands went to his waist. She tugged on his belt loops, pulling him closer.

"What do you say, cowboy?" she asked, her mouth against his. "You think you can handle a wild night?"

Could he ever have turned her down?

Hell, no.

He couldn't resist being with her, couldn't keep from wanting to take away that sad look he sometimes saw in her eyes. And, yeah, he wanted what she was offering before she left him for good: a repeat of the only time they'd been together.

But just because he couldn't refuse didn't mean he'd accept on her terms.

"A wild night?" He shook his head. "No. We've gotta watch that shoulder of yours, not to mention your head." He kissed her. "We'll take things slow—" he showed her that with another kiss "—and easy." He showed her how that would go, too.

After a few more demonstrations, they climbed into the truck and headed for home.

ON ANOTHER NIGHT, in another situation, the darkness of the truck might have tempted Carly to sleep.

Not tonight.

Luke's gaze at her from time to time and his hand on her skirt, his fingertips just brushing the bare skin of her thigh, kept her fully alert.

Heck, they kept her almost breathless with anticipation.

But when they arrived at his house and entered the kitchen, the wails coming from the direction of the living room told her their evening might have come to a screeching halt. Literally.

Tammy was pacing the living room floor, holding Luke's daughter in her arms. She looked wrung out. Rosie looked good for a few more hours.

Luke took the child and cuddled her close. She hiccupped a couple of times, stuck her finger in her mouth and put her head on his shoulder.

Carly's stomach twisted into a hard, little knot.

"She's being a handful," Tammy told them. "She won't take the teething ring and nothing else seems to satisfy her."

"She wants her daddy," Luke said.

So do I. Carly's cheeks burned at her instant response.

"I can stay if you'd like," Tammy offered. "I think it's going to be a long night."

"Thanks, but we're good. Rosie and I will get through it."

She nodded and picked up her bag from beside the couch. "Then I'll leave you all till tomorrow."

"I'll walk you out. Here, Carly." Luke handed the little girl over to her.

She had to reach up quickly to grab the child.

Luke and Tammy left the living room.

Rosie looked as stunned as Carly felt.

For a moment, they eyed each other in silence. Carly's heart beat so hard, she wondered if the baby could feel it.

Rosie's bottom lip quivered, her eyes opened wide and she let out an earsplitting wail.

Carly cringed. "Don't. Shh, shh. Baby, don't."

Huge tears ran down Rosie's cheeks. Carly reached up with the back of her hand to brush them away.

Rosie turned her head, opened her mouth and clamped down on Carly's finger. She stiffened as the child's few tiny teeth met her skin. But Rosie wasn't a bit interested in biting. Instead, she gummed Carly's knuckle, dribbling drool all over her hand.

Her heart thumped even harder, and her head spun.

Quickly, she sank to the edge of the couch, holding Rosie cradled against her.

They were still seated in that position, with Rosie occasionally struggling and letting loose a hiccupping wail, when Luke returned to the living room. He stopped in the doorway and smiled.

"Hey. You're a natural."

Carly blinked several times and took a shaky breath. "You might want to take her."

"Why? You're doing a great job."

But he crossed the room and lifted Rosie from her arms.

Carly took a tissue from her evening bag and wiped her hand.

"Yucky, huh?" Luke teased, sounding like five-year-old Alex.

"Very yucky," she agreed.

He took a seat beside her and cuddled Rosie against his chest. "All part of the territory. You'd know, if you had kids."

She choked on an indrawn breath and covered it with a cough.

"And to think I want to go through this again."

"Again?"

"More kids." He shook his head. "You know I'm an only child. My mom did a great job raising me, and we always had each other. But I always wanted a brother or sister or two. That's what I want for Rosie. Right, kiddo?"

Rosie answered with another wail.

"Someday," Luke said, "I'll give her a brother or sister. Or a couple of each. What about you?"

She froze. "Me? Kids? No," she fibbed, "I've never considered having kids. A family is not in my plans."

Rosie squirmed in his arms. "Hey, baby…" he murmured. He rose and began pacing the floor.

The irony of the situation made her want to groan in frustration. No matter her determination to part from Luke once and for all, after their kisses in the parking lot, she'd spent the ride back to the ranch hoping they would have some time alone.

As if he'd read her mind, Luke said, "Sorry about this. I didn't plan for the evening to turn out this way."

"Me, either." Her cheeks flamed. "But maybe it's better that it has."

Rosie wailed. Luke tilted his head away from her. "I wouldn't say that. Not at all. But I'm afraid Rosie's got other ideas." Smiling down at the baby, he nuzzled her cheek. "And when Rosie's hurting like this, she gets what she wants. Don't you, Daddy's little cowgirl?"

Carly choked. With the tissue clutched in one hand and her evening bag in the other, she rose to her feet. "I'd better go," she said, her voice shaking.

"She might calm down in a bit."

"No. I mean, maybe she will. But it's better I leave, anyhow. I…really, I went to dinner tonight for the chance to be alone with you. So I could tell you goodbye. I think it's best we just end things right now, instead of drawing them out."

Rosie screeched, no doubt in complete agreement.

And without another word, Carly fled.

Outside, she stumbled down the porch steps and made her way blindly across the yard. There was no full moon to guide her, as there had been the couple of nights she had walked home to the ranch house from Luke's. Now, in the darkness broken only by starlight, all she could see were the blurry outlines of the trees and the lighter patch of the path between them.

All she could hear was Luke's voice, calling Rosie "Daddy's little cowgirl."

All she could think of was the day he had come to the Roughneck, when he'd walked away after calling *her* that, too.

Since that day, she had heard the phrase over and over

again. The words had brought her nothing but heartache. And now…

Just moments ago she had heard him say those very words to his daughter.

And she realized how wrong she'd been for all these years. How easily she had thrown away her chance at happiness with him.

She would have found out the truth then, if only she hadn't been so ready to suspect him of other motives. So unable to believe someone could truly care about her.

So quick to take offense at what he'd called her— *Daddy's little cowgirl*—when he had never used the words as an insult at all.

Chapter Fourteen

"And how's our little girl today?" Tammy asked. Rosie sat in her high chair in the kitchen. Tammy ruffled her curls. "Feeling all better?"

"Seems to be," Luke said.

"How was last night?"

"Okay. She was up and down until about two."

"And how was the night with Carly?"

"Fine. She left right after you did."

Hell, she had run from the house as if every one of Rosie's stuffed animals had come to life and given chase.

And she'd left him damned unsatisfied.

When all was said and done, though, this morning he felt grateful. Her quick departure had kept him from becoming the world's biggest fool.

"I can keep Rosie overnight sometime, if you'd like."

He snapped his head up to look at his mother. She was giving him that wide-eyed innocent look he recognized from his growing-up days. But usually *he'd* been the one flashing it at *her*.

He spooned up another mouthful of applesauce and fed it to Rosie. Normally, she fed herself—or attempted to—but as overtired as she was today, she'd probably never hit her mouth. "What are you getting at, Mom?"

She slid onto a chair at the table and pushed aside one

of Rosie's storybooks. "Just that I know having Rosie around might cramp your style a bit."

At that, he laughed so heartily, Rosie looked at him in surprise, then joined in. "I don't have a style to be cramped. What you see is what you get. And what I see is what I've got, and I'm lucky to have her." He aimed another spoonful at his daughter's mouth. "Rosie comes first."

That's the way it was…no matter how much he might be attracted to Carly.

And, though he hated to admit it, even to himself, he was way beyond attracted. Not that he planned to do anything about it now.

"I told you the other day, she needs a mama."

"Mom. No more. If you're trying to lead up to nominating Carly Baron for the job, you can forget it."

"Why? Obviously you're interested in her, or you wouldn't have taken her out."

"That won't be an issue in the future."

Her mouth opened and closed again. She might encourage and cajole and even give him a push once in a while, but she wouldn't outright tell him what to do. Still, he saw the curiosity in her eyes. Best to nip it in the bud right now, along with any other thoughts she might have of him getting together with Carly.

"You're right. I need a wife and a mom for Rosie. But Carly doesn't want kids."

"Where did you hear that?"

"From the lady herself."

"I can't believe it."

"Why? Not everybody's cut out to be a great mom, like you."

She smiled. "Flattery will get you everywhere. Why don't you try some with Carly?"

He rolled his eyes. After wiping Rosie's mouth and hands, he took the applesauce bowl to the sink to rinse it. "Time for me to head over to the barn. We've got that mare ready to foal any day now, and I want to keep an eye on her."

A minute later, he left the house, shaking his head over their entire conversation.

Parenting advice from Brock Baron and now relationship advice from his mom. Since when had his life gotten turned so upside-down?

Since Carly Baron had walked back into it.

He would just have to let her walk right back out again.

He traveled the well-worn path to the barn, his thoughts pushing him to a furious pace.

Tammy was right. Rosie needed a mama, and that was a role Carly could never fill.

She had come right out and told him she didn't want a family. With that statement, she had ended any chance they would ever have for a relationship.

And still, as he strode into the barn and tried to focus on the business of the day ahead of him, he couldn't stop his thoughts from straying to her.

He should have realized her feelings about having kids long before now. Maybe he would have, if part of his anatomy hadn't taken over his good sense. He knew her history, had heard plenty about how she felt growing up in a large family, recalled the many times she'd told him about how she hated feeling lost in the crowd.

She didn't want kids. Or a relationship.

Yet there was no denying she had been as hot for him last night as he was for her.

Didn't take long for *her* to cool.

Focus.

He made sure the pile of tack he'd seen on the workbench before he'd left last night had been cleaned, sorted and rehung. He stopped to inspect a horse the vet had been treating for an infected leg wound. Done with that he went to the far stall to check on the pregnant mare.

"Luke!"

It was Carly. He stepped out of the stall.

She stood in the wide doorway, the sunshine streaming in from behind, making her blond hair glow, outlining every curve of her body. The take-charge part of his anatomy jumped to attention.

Damn. When would *he* cool down, too?

Then she called his name again. He frowned.

Her voice sounded odd—high, tight, as if she'd lost control of her breathing.

Carly looked down the length of the barn and took a long, steadying breath.

When she had finished talking to Savannah and Travis, her first thought had been to find Luke, and the first place she checked was the barn.

She shouldn't have come here. She knew it.

Yet she couldn't stay away.

"Luke!" She almost tripped over her own feet in her eagerness to reach him.

He put both his hands on her arms, steadying her. "What's wrong?"

She shook her head, unable to speak for the emotions running through her. She heaved a deep breath and let it out again. "Nothing's wrong. Travis found Genevieve Caron."

His eyes widened in astonishment.

"She's Genevieve Lewis now. She lives in Lubbock. I talked to her on the phone."

"She remembered you?"

"She did. We didn't get into much detail and she doesn't know where my mom is now. But I'm going to go see her tomorrow night." Her voice broke, and she lowered it to a shaky whisper. "It sounded as if she might have more current info that could get us closer to finding my mom."

He gave her a quick bear hug that warmed her from head to toe. Then he stood back, smiling down at her. "Carly, that's great news."

"It is." Her pulse raced. She'd walked out on him last night, and still he was happy for her. His support thrilled her. And so did he.

When she had left the Peach Pit and headed home, she told herself she wanted to see Luke only because she had no one else to share her news with.

That was a lie. But she couldn't worry about it right now.

Before she could second-guess the action, she threw herself into his arms. This hug made her even warmer. But then, it wasn't nearly as quick as the first one.

Luke's arms went around her again, holding her close. Raising herself on tiptoe, she slid her body another inch or two up the length of his. She tilted her head back to look at him and reached up to thread her fingers through his hair, not giving a darn when she knocked his Stetson to the ground.

He didn't seem to mind.

She tugged, urging his head downward.

That didn't appear to bother him, either.

He took her mouth with his, gently at first, then with increasing pressure, his lips tasting, tongue exploring, teeth nibbling at her lower lip.

She touched her tongue to his. He groaned and shifted his feet, moving to brace her against the adjacent stall door. She was pinned in place by his hips, but her hands were free to roam. She ran her fingertips across his shoulders and down his chest, slipped her arms around him and pulled him close, the way he had held her.

There was no escaping the effect she had on his body. No denying her thrill at the knowledge.

She lifted her chin to look up at him. He bent and put his mouth to her throat. Even as his kiss tickled her sensitive skin, it sent shivers of pleasure all through her.

She tilted her head—and froze. "Um...Luke."

"What?" He trailed his lips across her throat, making her shiver again.

"Luke, stop." She pushed against his muscled arms, tried and failed to hold back a giggle. "We've got an audience."

His head whipped up, almost catching her chin. He turned to look in the direction she was staring. Though he was still taking deep, unsteady breaths and seemed annoyed as heck at the interruption, even he couldn't help but laugh.

Framed in the opening of the next stall, Daredevil stood watching them.

THE SUMMONS FROM Brock late in the morning didn't surprise Luke. He'd expected the boss would want to go over the equipment order he had turned in yesterday.

Brock's gesture to close the door of the den seemed stiff and abrupt. His face looked lined with strain. That trip to the Peach Pit the other day without his wheelchair must have taken a toll.

Carly had been right about that.

Not something Brock would want to hear.

"I brought a copy of the equipment list—"

"Forget the list."

Luke fought to keep his brows from rising at the snapped response.

Brock slapped his hands on the arms of the wheelchair. "This is not about the damned list. This is about what the hell went on in my barn this morning."

Crap.

Daredevil hadn't been the only one taking in the show.

"What the hell did you think you were doing messing around with my daughter?"

"You were there?"

"Damn right I was there. Standing outside the barn door. You're lucky I didn't call you out right then." Brock glared. He'd had all day to get himself worked up into this rage. The fallout wasn't going to be pretty. "And what does it matter whether or not I was there to witness your shenanigans? Do you think if I hadn't seen you with my own eyes, if I'd gotten my knowledge secondhand, you could bluff your way out of trouble with a pack of lies?"

"No, I don't think that. I've never lied to you before and wouldn't start now."

Brock made a derisive sound. "That remains to be seen. But that's not my point. What I want to know is, what the hell were you doing with your hands all over my little girl?"

Luke stood his ground, arms at his sides, his Stetson in one hand. He would tell the truth about this, too. The boss wasn't going to like his reply. "She's not a little girl anymore, Brock. And her hands were as busy as mine."

A blue vein ticked in the man's forehead. His face turned red. His eyes glittered. "You're done," he said between clenched teeth. He slammed his hand on the desktop. "You've got one week to clear out of here."

Luke stared back at him. His fingers tightened on the

Stetson's brim. "You haven't got just cause to fire me for this. Carly and I are both adults. But she's your daughter, and you've got to do as you see fit." He shrugged. "Hell. I love Rosie as much as you love Carly. And I admit, in your shoes, I'd probably do the same."

Chapter Fifteen

Feeling ridiculously apprehensive, Carly knocked on Luke's front door. A moment later, from inside, she heard footsteps on the hardwood floor. The small diamond-shaped pane of glass in the door showed her a flash of blond hair and pink fabric. Her shoulders sagged. She had hoped Luke would be there.

By the time Tammy swung the door open, Carly had a smile plastered on her face. "Hi."

"Hi, Carly. Come on in." Tammy closed the door behind them. "But I'm afraid Luke's not home yet."

"I came to ask how Rosie was feeling."

"See for yourself." Tammy gestured to the other side of the room.

Rosie lay sprawled on the floor with her head pillowed on her favorite stuffed elephant, fast asleep.

"She's doing fine now," Tammy told her. "But the poor kid's worn out. She was up most of last night." She took a seat on the couch. On the coffee table in front of her sat a coffee mug and a magazine, its cover and first few pages curled under. "Please, have a seat."

Carly sat on the edge of a large brown chair that matched the couch.

"You haven't been seeing our girl at her best, unfortunately," Tammy continued. "Not that she's always a perfect angel, but this has been a particularly bad week. Teething takes a lot out of kids."

"Does it?"

"Yes, especially if they run a fever with it. You'll find that out for yourself one day, I'm sure."

Carly's fingers tightened on the shopping bag she was carrying. "I...I was hoping Rosie would feel better by now." She set the bag on the broad, flat arm of the upholstered chair. "I brought something for her. It's a toy I used to play with when I was a kid."

"Well, that's awfully nice of you."

She pulled the small plastic terrier puppy from the sack. "Buster was always one of my favorites. I found him in the attic with some of my old things and gave him a good scrub." She smiled. "He barks when you squeeze his stomach."

Tammy smiled back at her. "Rosie will love that. You can give it to her yourself, if she wakes up while you're still here." She sat back against the couch cushion. "Luke called earlier to say he had a lot of work he wanted to clear up. I'm not sure what time he'll be home, but I shouldn't think he'll be much longer."

"I don't need to stay. I'll just leave Buster here for Rosie."

"Actually..." Tammy stared at her.

She tensed, not sure what was behind the woman's suddenly thoughtful expression.

"I have a couple of errands I need to run. I didn't mention them to Luke. He sounded so distracted when he called. But it would be a big help if I could take care of them tonight. I hate to ask you, but do you think you could stay till he gets here?"

"Stay?" Carly tightened her grip on the puppy, who

gave his well-remembered little squeaky bark. "With Rosie, you mean?"

Tammy nodded. "I would never leave her with someone she doesn't know, but you're not a stranger to her, are you?"

Yes, I am. She's only seen me a few times.

But how could she reject a request for such a simple favor? And Tammy must know she had planned to stay a little while, or why else would she have come in and taken a seat?

She found herself nodding and saying, "Sure. I'm happy to wait with Rosie."

"Wonderful." Tammy stood. "Let me put her to bed. Come on, I'll show you where her crib is." Gently, she lifted the sleeping little girl into her arms and carried her from the room.

Carly followed, already sure she knew which bedroom Rosie would occupy—the smaller of the two, the one on the left of the hallway, on the same wall as the bathroom. The previous ranch manager, a bachelor, had used that room as his den.

With a handful of wall decals, Luke or Tammy or both had turned the space into a cartoon jungle. A monkey swung from a banana tree on one wall, and a herd of long-necked giraffes stalked across another. Even the sheets of the crib were decorated with a row of marching elephants, each with his trunk curled around the stubby tail of the one before him.

Carly laughed softly. "No wonder Rosie likes her stuffed animals so much."

"Yes," Tammy said, setting the little girl onto the crib mattress and tucking a soft-looking pink rabbit against her. "Luke can't wait till she graduates to horses. He wanted to decorate with them right away, but I talked him out of it."

"I love horses, too," Carly told her, "but these animals are perfect for a baby."

"That's just what I told him."

They both smiled. Tammy flicked on a small night-light on a white wicker chest.

Carly followed her back to the living room.

"She's already been fed and changed. Her teething ring is on the door of the refrigerator, if you need it. Thanks so much for staying with her."

And before Carly could blink, Tammy had taken her mug from the coffee table and left the room again. Only moments later, she heard the sound of running water, then the back door closing.

She was alone in the house with Rosie. Alone in the living room. At least, until Luke came home.

At the thought, her heart skipped a beat. She shouldn't have come here. Not after the way she had run away from him last night. Not even after the way she had kissed him in the barn this morning. Not when she had finally convinced herself she could stay away.

Buster sat on the coffee table where she had left him. She picked up the toy and squeezed gently, smiling at his squeaky bark.

Upstairs in the ranch house that afternoon, she had taken Buster from his packing box and turned to leave the attic. Her foot had struck something on the floor. When she bent to look, she found the ribbon-wrapped bundle of envelopes.

Love letters from Luke.

A small bundle, appropriately enough, since they had dated for such a short time. But that bundle was huge in its impact on her life. Each note was filled with sweet nothings and simple chatter. Each was signed, "Love you, Luke."

Leaving that bundle behind when she went away to college was the toughest thing she had ever done…up to that point in her life.

When she had come home for the first time after learning she was pregnant, she had wanted to look for the letters but found the will to resist. After she lost the baby, she wouldn't let herself think of those love letters. Or the man who had written them.

This afternoon, alone in her room, she had read that final "Love you, Luke."

Those words had brought her to him again tonight. Maybe she should have taken his absence as an omen that she'd made the wrong choice.

Trying to distract herself, she grabbed the women's magazine Tammy had left lying on the coffee table. She hadn't gotten through a third of the pages before she heard a cry from down the hall.

As she got up from the couch, Rosie cried out again.

To her own surprise, she recognized the sound wasn't an urgent summons. It wasn't a wail or a yowl, like those she remembered from the other night. The small noise was only meant to call attention to the fact that Rosie was awake and wanted attention.

Still, she stood in the doorway of the little girl's bedroom filled with as much trepidation as when she had knocked on Luke's front door.

Rosie stood in the crib, her little hands fisted around two of the upright slats, looking like a prison inmate clutching the bars of her cell. Carly couldn't hold back a smile.

To her shock, Rosie grinned back at her. She bounced

up and down a couple of times on the mattress, then reached between the slats, holding her arms out.

She wanted to be taken from the crib.

Carly swallowed hard and crossed her arms over her chest. She hadn't planned on having to deal with Rosie after Tammy left. She had expected the little girl to stay fast asleep.

An all-too-wide-awake Rosie threw herself against the wooden crib as if trying to extend her arms toward Carly. She gave a grunting cry. Even Carly's untrained ear could hear the sound of frustration.

Now would Rosie give way to what she had feared the other night? Tears? Screams, maybe? Even a full-fledged tantrum?

That night, Luke had been there with her. Now, she reminded herself, she was on her own. If Rosie's cries escalated, who knew what it would take to calm her?

The thought was enough to send her across the room to lift the little girl from her crib.

Rosie reached up to pat her cheeks with both hands. She seemed to wait for a response Carly didn't know how to make. After a moment, the little girl evidently gave up. Leaning forward, she rested her head on Carly's shoulder and snuggled against her.

Arms stiff, Carly held Luke's child.

Soft curls brushed her jaw. The scent of baby powder washed over her. Warmth from the little body seemed to seep into her chest and spread through her heart.

A rush of tears blurred her vision. She closed her eyes, cuddled Rosie closer and, her heart hammering beneath her breastbone, thought of her own child.

"I almost had a baby like you, Rosie," she whispered.

Rosie rubbed her face against Carly's neck, as if offering sympathy and unspoken support.

"I carried my baby for sixteen weeks. That's four months. That's a long time. Long enough for me to know how much I wanted to be a mommy." Her sigh ruffled Rosie's curls. "I don't even know if it was a boy or a girl. But I know I loved my baby. Just the way your daddy loves you."

Rosie lay still, content.

Even in the semidarkness of the bedroom, with the child asleep in her arms, she couldn't whisper the rest of what she had never confessed to anyone.

How she had lost the baby she loved.

And how much she feared Luke, who loved his own little girl, would hate her if he ever discovered the truth.

Carly rocked the child against her, then began to walk the floor. Light and even and untroubled, Rosie's breath tickled her neck. She cupped one hand around the back of the baby's head, holding her close.

So precious. So little now. But year after year, Rosie would grow bigger, would go to preschool, move on to kindergarten. Would graduate from grade school and go on to high school.

Luke wouldn't miss a moment. He would have another wall cabinet full of photos, with all the new stages of Rosie's development displayed for all to see.

Any daddy would burst with pride at watching his little girl grow up.

Any mommy ought to feel the same.

But she hadn't been given her chance to be that mommy. And her own mother, who'd had the chance, had thrown it—and her children—away.

Fresh tears filled her eyes.

Without a murmur, Rosie slept on.

Her crib stood empty. Her bunny sat waiting to be tucked in.

And still, with Rosie's warm little body cuddled against her, Carly paced the floor.

LUKE WALKED BACK to the house long after his usual arrival time, expecting to find Tammy dealing with an uncontrollable Rosie.

Instead, he discovered her car gone and Carly sitting on the living room couch in tears.

He froze in the doorway. "What happened? Where's Rosie? And Mom?"

She wiped her face with the back of her hand and shook her head frantically, her hair tumbling around her shoulders. "No, it's okay," she said in a rush, "they're fine. Rosie's asleep. I brought her a toy. Your mom had some errands to run and asked me to stay." She dabbed at her eyes with a crumpled tissue.

Despite that kiss in the barn, after the way she had run from the house last night, he'd never expected to see her here again.

She'd brought Rosie a toy.

He saw the dog beside her on the couch. Feeling both elated and confused, he crossed the living room toward her. "What's wrong?"

"Nothing." Staring ahead of her, she drew her legs up onto the couch and wrapped her arms around them.

He got the message. She didn't want him near. Instead of taking the seat beside her as he'd planned, he dropped onto the chair beside the couch. "How can it be nothing when you're sitting here crying your eyes out?"

She rested her chin on her knees. "I was…I was thinking about my mom and…and everything just got to me, I guess."

"'Everything'?"

"The meeting with Mrs. Lewis tomorrow. It might

come to nothing, as you said, I know that. But it might come to something, too. It might lead to my mom. And I started thinking what that could mean." Her eyes looked huge and glittery. "Ever since she left, I've dreamed up scenarios of how it would be when I finally saw her again. When I finally got to ask her why she left us. And now, one of those scenarios might come true."

And all the stories she'd told herself, he'd bet, came with the standard happily-ever-after ending.

He didn't want to be the one to burst that happiness bubble. He also didn't want to see her crushed if things didn't work out the way she'd dreamed. But life seldom worked out exactly the way folks planned.

"It might be a new scenario altogether," he said, keeping his voice low. "Maybe one you've never thought of before."

"Maybe. Mrs. Lewis said they've lost contact with each other," she admitted. "But they were still in touch after Mom left the Roughneck. She'll have more recent information than anything we've been able to turn up."

"You said she lives in Lubbock?"

"A few miles outside of it. We're meeting at her house, tomorrow night."

"That's a five-hour trip." A long ride there, keyed up by years of anticipation. A longer ride home, if the news wasn't good.

"I don't mind the drive. It was the earliest she could meet with me. And the next day, she's going out of town for a while." She crumpled the tissue and shoved it into her jeans pocket. "I wasn't about to wait till she got home again."

"Is Savannah going with you?"

"No. I'll stay overnight somewhere in Lubbock."

"I'll go with you."

She sat up straight, her eyes wide again. "That's not necessary."

"Somebody needs to go with you."

"No one knows about the search but Savannah. And Travis. I don't need anyone with me. But thanks."

"I'm going. And you don't have to thank me."

"You can't just walk off for an overnight stay. You've got a ranch to run."

Not for very much longer. But she didn't need to know that.

He'd stayed late tonight to finish up some of his current paperwork. He had no backlog, no unfinished business. His files were all up-to-date. His men had the barn and the tack inspection-ready and all the equipment in good working order. The furniture here came with the house. He'd need to move only Rosie's crib and their personal belongings.

Getting fired that afternoon had stunned him, but it wouldn't keep him from leaving everything in top shape or making sure his departure was quick and smooth. Pride wouldn't let him have things any other way.

He smiled. "I'm ready for a day off." What was one day, anyhow, when he'd soon have more free time than he'd ever wanted, until he could line up another job?

"Really, you don't need to go with me. You've got a… You've got Rosie to worry about."

"Mom can keep her overnight. Or stay here, if it's easier. She's done it before." He leaned forward, resting his forearms on his knees. He kept his voice low again. "Carly, I don't want to keep throwing negatives at you, and I sure as hell hope your talk with Mrs. Lewis has a positive outcome. But I see how you are tonight, after just thinking about what you might learn." He shook his head. "I'm not letting you walk into that meeting alone."

Chapter Sixteen

In twenty years, Genevieve Lewis hadn't changed much. The bright red hair of the stick figure in Carly's pictures had faded a bit and become threaded with silver. The face had softened some compared to the memories triggered by those hand-drawn pictures. Other than that, Carly felt sure she would have known the woman if she'd met her on the street.

On the other hand, Carly had changed so much Mrs. Lewis didn't recognize her when she opened the door to them. "Except for your eyes. You do have Brock Baron's eyes."

They were seated in the living room—the parlor, she called it—with steaming cups of tea on the table in front of them.

Carly hadn't wanted the tea or the plate of cookies their hostess set out. She and Luke had arrived early in Lubbock, found a place to stay for the night and then gone for dinner.

She'd been too keyed up to eat much, both from anticipating the upcoming meeting with Mrs. Lewis and from the knowledge that, afterward, she and Luke would spend the night together. He'd taken only one room at the motel…though it did have two double beds.

Carly sipped at her hot tea and attempted to get con-

trol of her thoughts. This meeting was too important
for her not to have focus. "You know my daddy, too,
Mrs. Lewis?"

The other woman nodded. "Yes. Not very well,
though. Most of the time, I visited Delia at the house during the day, when he was working. It was just your mama
and you and your brother at home then. And Anna."

"You know my mom...left the ranch when I was five."

"Yes." She looked down at her teacup. "I did tell you
on the phone that we've lost touch and I haven't heard
from her in years now."

"You did," Carly assured her. "But, as I'd said, I'm
trying to find out where she is now. And to contact her.
Anything you can tell me might help."

She nodded. "Well, when I lived in Dallas, I visited
her at the ranch often. My younger son was already in
high school and gone all day. With four children, Delia
didn't go far from home very often. But she enjoyed
company, always liked having folks around her. And
she loved to throw a party."

Carly looked at her in surprise. "I remember family
birthday parties from when I was young. I can't place
my mom at any of them." Her voice shook. Luke put his
hand over hers. She grasped his fingers, letting the sol-
idness of him help to steady her.

She hadn't wanted him to come with her on this trip.
She knew she had to keep her distance from him. Her
time with Rosie had only reinforced the wisdom of that.
But now she felt grateful he'd insisted on accompany-
ing her.

"We don't have photos from those early parties."
Something she had never found odd till now.

"Maybe Brock destroyed any pictures from that time,"

Mrs. Lewis said gently. "He might have thought you children would be hurt by seeing photos of Delia."

By having reminders of the mom who was no longer in their lives.

And yet, the description Mrs. Lewis had given didn't sound like a woman who would close herself off from people or walk away from her family.

"When you were about four," the woman continued, "my husband passed away. I relocated here to be closer to my oldest son, who lives in Lubbock. In the year after that, I didn't see Delia as often. But I still visited."

"Did she seem any different to you that last year? Or in the few years just before?"

"She was a little more tired, maybe. That was all."

Tired. Or depressed.

"Did you know she was planning to leave the ranch?"

Mrs. Lewis shook her head. "I had no idea she wasn't still living in Dallas until one day when I received a note from her in the mail."

"Did she say anything to explain what made her leave?"

"No, she didn't."

"But you knew she wasn't at the Roughneck anymore. Did she say where she was living?"

"She was staying with a friend. Not someone I knew. And after all this time, I don't remember her name."

"What about the note?" Luke asked. "Can you recall the address she'd mailed it from or even the postmark?"

"It was still in Texas, that I do know. It might've been San Antonio. But I can't say for sure."

"Would you still have the note?" Carly asked.

"Oh, I doubt it. That was twenty years ago. And when I downsized, I got rid of so much old correspondence." She considered for a moment. "My son has been storing

a few boxes for me for a while. For years now, actually."
She laughed. "I turned the tables, didn't I? It's usually
the parents who hold on to things for their kids."

"Usually. That's how I knew to get in touch with
you—from something I'd stored away in the attic." She
thought of Luke's letters to her and had to force a smile.
"Is it possible you might have the note somewhere in
those boxes?"

"I wouldn't think so."

Her heart sank.

"Although," Mrs. Lewis added thoughtfully, "I remember your mama always sent lovely Christmas cards,
and I'm a great one for saving pretty cards. I always
planned to do something crafty with them. That would
be more of a possibility than the note, I'm sure."

Carly tightened her fingers around Luke's. "Would
you be able to take a look?"

"Of course, I would. I'm going to be away, visiting my
younger son. I'll check once I get back, if that's all right."

She swallowed a sigh of disappointment. "That would
be great."

"But I would hate to raise your hopes for no reason."
A worry line appeared above Mrs. Lewis's eyes. "I can't
swear that I'll have saved any of the cards, or even if I
did, that I kept the envelopes."

"I understand."

"Carly mentioned you'd been in touch with Delia after
she left the Roughneck," Luke said. "Did you mean the
Christmas cards, or did you have other contact with her?"

"I saw her a few times. She visited me here. And we
met once in Lubbock for dinner. That was a while after
she had left the ranch."

"Is there anything you can remember from those visits?" Carly asked. "Any details about…about her new life that she might have mentioned?"

"No, not that I can recall. I've been thinking about it since your phone call yesterday, and I haven't come up with anything. Delia didn't seem to want to discuss the present at all. We talked mostly of the past, about my boys, and you and Jet and your sisters."

Carly clenched her free hand by her side. As if he knew how Mrs. Lewis's statement had affected her, Luke squeezed her hand and brushed his thumb across her knuckles.

"I'm sorry I haven't been more helpful."

"No need to be sorry at all, Mrs. Lewis," she said sincerely. "You've given me hope of getting an address. I know it's a faint hope but, still, it's more than we've been able to find."

The woman nodded. "Maybe your daddy will remember something else to help you, too."

"Something else?"

"Yes. I don't know if Delia kept in touch with him or not after they met in Fort Worth, but if so, maybe the name of the friend she stayed with will come to him."

Carly sat back in surprise, her shoulders pressed so firmly against the couch, pain bolted down her arm. "They met in Fort Worth," she repeated flatly. "You mean, after my mom left home?"

"Yes. As I mentioned, she and I had dinner in Lubbock. That night, she told me she planned to see Brock."

ON THE WAY back to the motel, Carly had been so incensed that Luke expected to see scorch marks inside the truck's cab. He didn't altogether blame her. From what Mrs. Lewis had told them, it seemed possible Brock

Baron had once deliberately denied his kids the chance to reconnect with their mom.

In their motel room, she dropped her duffel bag on the floor and shoved it over near the wall, out of the way. She leaned back against the dresser, crossing her arms and looking in his direction. He wondered if she actually saw him.

"I should have gone right back home tonight," she muttered.

"We can leave now, if you want. But it would be two a.m., at the earliest, before we'd get to Dallas. Better to get a good night's sleep and take the trip home in the morning."

After you've had some time to calm down.

Her next words proved the foolishness of *that* thought.

"Whenever I get there, I'm going to tear into Daddy. He saw my mom, Luke. And he never said anything to anyone."

He set his duffel down on the nearest bed and took a seat beside it. They might be in for a long night—and not the kind he'd looked forward to. "Has your daddy ever talked to you or Savannah or anyone about Delia?"

After a long, tense pause, she admitted, "Not that I know of." Her words sounded brittle.

Taking his life in his hands, he said gently, "Then, it's probably a good idea not to jump to conclusions."

"*Jump to conclusions?* You heard Mrs. Lewis—he saw my mom after she left us."

"No. Mrs. Lewis said Delia was planning to see your daddy. But she didn't know when or where, and she hasn't seen your mom since the night they met for dinner. There's no proof your mom followed through on her statement. Or that Brock agreed to the meet."

"Of course you'd take his side. He's your—"

"Don't go there." That time, he couldn't keep his tone gentle. Couldn't believe she'd throw the job in his face. Again. "I'm not taking anybody's side in this. I'm trying to get you to see the truth."

She raked her hand through her hair and paced across the room, away from him. "I'm sorry. I didn't mean what I said. It's not you I'm furious with, it's my daddy."

She paced back toward him. Her eyes blazed. From anger, obviously. And, he suspected, from hurt.

He watched her stomp away again.

Whatever Brock might've held back from his family, she saw it as another betrayal.

Just the way she had felt he betrayed her.

No matter what she did or didn't mean to bring up, she'd been going to throw her accusation at him again. He could hang on to a lot of hurt of his own about that, if he cared to dwell on it. But right now all he could think of was Carly. He needed to calm her down. Or… maybe not.

By the time she swung his way again, he had risen to stand in her path. She stumbled to a halt in front of him. Her chest heaved and her eyes sparkled and color brightened her cheeks.

As he stood there for a moment, saying nothing, the pinkness in her cheeks deepened.

He tried a smile. "We're here for the night. Why don't we do something to get you through it?"

"Like what?"

"Like picking up where we left off in the barn yesterday and seeing how far we get this time."

After a moment's hesitation, she put her hands on her hips and cocked her head.

The wild-girl act. Well, if that was what she needed to get her mind off her troubles, she could go for it.

"Daredevil's not here to see us, is he?" she said.

Neither is your daddy.

What the hell did that matter? A week from now, his employment at the Roughneck would be just a line on a job application.

He reached out to tug Carly toward him, but she beat him to it, wrapping her arms around his neck the way she'd done in the barn.

She kissed him as though the night would last forever.

He kissed her as though he hadn't a care in the world about next week.

When they finally came up for air, he smiled and reached for the top snap of her pink Western shirt. "Ready to show me your slow, sexy ride?"

"I told you once before," she said, her breath coming in gasps, "that's for city slickers."

"Oh, no," he objected. "Not the kind of riding I've got in mind."

Before he could go for the next snap on her shirt, she had popped them all in one swift yank. She reached for the button on her jeans.

He'd hoped for the pleasure of undressing her himself. But, hell, that could wait for the next time. Not to be outdone, he got to work on his own shirt, belt buckle and jeans.

By then, she'd climbed onto the bed and was reaching for the sheet.

He took her hand. "No. I want to see everything I've missed all these years."

The light seeping around the motel room drapes showed him the pale perfection of her skin, highlighted by the contrast of twin pink nipples, already pebbled and waiting for him, and a tangled mound of soft blond curls. His body hardened, and his heartbeat thundered in his chest.

He should let her take the lead, let her unload her anger with some hot, energetic sex. Why not, when working out her aggressions was only going to bring them both to satisfaction?

Then she bit her lip, and all thoughts of giving her control went by the wayside.

That flash of uncertainty and the faint vulnerability he'd always been able to see in her eyes did him in. No matter what mask she liked to hide behind, beneath it she was still his same sweet Carly.

He tossed the covers far out of reach and slid onto the bed beside her. He caught both her hands with one of his and tugged gently upward, resting her hands above her head on the pillow, curving his fingers to encircle her wrists. Her eyes widened. Her lips parted. He didn't wait for the words. He took her mouth, covering it with his, teasing her with his tongue until they were both gasping for breath again.

He worked his way slowly downward, kissing her from lips to hips, taking care to honor the highlights he'd seen just a short while ago.

She bucked against him like an untamed colt testing a restraining lasso. He didn't have the damned strength to draw this teasing out any longer. He wanted the freedom of his release as much as she wanted hers.

But not nearly as much as he simply wanted her.

He scooped her up in his arms, feeling the much-welcome torture of her body pressed against his. He slid his hands down to cup her hips, then watched with pure pleasure as she rose to straddle him.

"All right, cowgirl," he urged. "Let's see you go wild."

Chapter Seventeen

Carly woke to find Luke lying with his leg across her hips and his hand resting possessively at her waist.

The bedside clock read 1:00 a.m. The lights outside the motel came through the chinks around the drapes, making it seem as though a few weak rays of the sun were trying to creep inside.

She lay there, knowing she was bare except where Luke touched her, feeling wonderfully tender in a few places and fighting the hot blush that rose to her cheeks.

Last night, they had made love, and it had been as wild as she had promised him the night they'd made out in the restaurant parking lot after their dinner date. *She* had been as wild as Luke had encouraged her to be. The hot blush went up a few degrees.

Only now did she think about how wrong this had been.

Not the lovemaking or the sex or the anger displacement or whatever they should call it. But the fact that she'd slept with Luke, all the while knowing this couldn't last—no matter how much she wanted it to.

He brushed her belly with his thumb.

Startled, she turned her head.

He lay watching her, his mouth curved in a smile.

"You're blushing," he said. "What are you thinking about?"

"How hot it is in here."

"Or about how hot it was in here last night?"

"Was it?"

"It was for me, thanks to you." He reached up to run his finger along her jaw. "Now it's time for what I promised you."

"What would that be?" But she knew, and at the thought alone, her body responded all the way down to her toes.

"Slow and easy," he said.

In the parking lot, he'd shown her with his kisses. Now, he showed her with his hands and body, too.

As they lay together afterward, he spooned himself around her and held her tight.

She stared straight ahead at the green-and-gold motel wallpaper and a picture mounted on the wall. The gilt frame made her think of the curio cabinets in his living room.

He kissed her shoulder, and a shiver went down her spine. She was warm and cozy and…feeling as though Luke really cared.

And she was keeping something from him that he had always had the right to know.

She sat up and reached across the space between the two beds to grab the nearest piece of clothing she could find—the blue Western shirt with white snaps and trim she'd watched Luke tear off last night before joining her on the bed. She slipped her arms into the sleeves and held the shirt tightly around her, the way he had just been holding her and never would again.

The tails of his shirt fell modestly to her knees, but still she shivered. She reached for the sheet and blanket.

Smiling, Luke propped himself up on one elbow. "You should have told me you'd gotten cold. I would have warmed you up."

"Not this kind of cold." Nothing could take away this bone-deep chill. Nothing could quiet the emotions raging through her, especially the guilt that weighed more heavily on her than the bedclothes she'd just tugged up to her waist. She rested her head against the headboard and sighed.

Luke sat up to face her. "What's wrong?"

"I don't know how to begin."

"You're still upset about what we heard from Mrs. Lewis last night."

It was as good a place as any to start. "About my daddy knowing something? Yes, I'm upset. But you're right about not jumping to conclusions. I can't be sure of what happened. Yet. For now, I'm more upset that we didn't get a definite lead."

"Yet," he repeated. "She might turn up an address for you."

"I know. I'm trying not to be too impatient, not to expect more than that. But I've got so much wrapped up in finding my mom. So many issues from my childhood I hope she can help me resolve." So many questions about her mom's abandonment, her emotions…and her possible struggle with depression…

She sighed, her breath catching. "My family always called me the wild child, and it gave me something to hang on to, to hide what I was really feeling." She paused for a long moment. "I'm not like that in Houston. Not like that at all anymore. But since I came back home this last time and saw you again, I've been trying to hide by pretending to be that wild girl again."

"I know," he said.

Surprised, she glanced at him, then looked away. Beneath the covers, she drew her knees up and wrapped her arms around them. "It's not working, though. Maybe I needed the reputation when I was a kid, but I don't want it to hang over my future." She sighed again. "There's a lot of baggage I'd like to leave behind from back then. Luke, I made a mistake that day you came to the ranch, and I so regret it."

"I know. We've talked about it."

"But it's more than just regret. I was only a teen—a hurt teen—and I blurted out what I did to hurt you, too. I don't want you to suffer because of my mistake."

"I haven't. If I'd let that day hang over me, I'd never have taken the manager's job at the Roughneck. A job," he added with slow emphasis, "that your daddy offered me."

She looked at him again.

"That's right." His expression seemed sad. "You thought, when I quit rodeo, I went to the ranch again, looking for work. Instead, Brock came looking for me."

"I'm sorry. I guess I haven't changed much from that hurt teen."

"You've changed. A lot." He rested his hand on her blanket-covered knee. "And you've never been a wild girl to me. I've always seen who you really are—a girl looking for a place to belong. Finding your mom isn't going to help with that. It's something you need to figure out on your own. And I have to tell you, I don't think you'll do that through bull riding."

Her laugh sounded more like a sob. "I'm sure I won't. A few rides on Twister were enough to tell me that."

"Finding where you belong isn't as hard as you think, Carly. You only need to make up your mind about where you'd be happiest. The way I decided my place isn't with the rodeo, but with Rosie."

She could barely force herself to admit, "I wish my mom had cared about us the way you love Rosie."

"She's everything."

The simple declaration broke her. She swallowed hard, fighting for control, searching for the way to tell him what she needed to share. There was no easy way. She could only tell him the truth.

"My first months away at school, I missed my family. I missed Kim. But most of all, I missed you."

"You never contacted me."

"How could I, after the way we split up?" Her voice broke. "I stayed away from home as long as I could, but when I came back on fall break, I needed to see you."

"I was easy enough to find."

"You and Jodi. I heard you were always together, and had been since the summer. Since not long after you and I broke up. So I left again, without telling you—" a tear ran down her cheek and she dashed it away "—without telling you I was pregnant."

His hand tightened on her knee. *"What?"* He stared into space, and she knew he was rapidly doing the math, counting the weeks from their night in the desert. "You knew before you left for school?"

"No. Not before. But," she admitted, "I found out not long after I got to Houston."

He cursed under his breath. "Why didn't you get in touch with me right away?"

She shrugged. "Hurt teen, again. I didn't think you would care. And I couldn't tell anyone else. My daddy would have killed me. The rest of the family would have just chalked it up to my being wild."

After what seemed like an hour, he said quietly, "And the baby?"

The most difficult part for her to share. "Right after I went back from the break, I competed in a fall rodeo. A couple of weeks later, I started spotting." Tears fell so rapidly, she gave up trying to brush them away. "I was sixteen weeks along when I lost the baby. The doctor said it probably wasn't from competing but—" Her voice broke.

He took her into his arms. "Then you've got to believe what the doctor said."

"But he told me there was a chance. A chance that what I'd done made me lose the baby. He said we'll never know for sure."

He wrapped her in a hug. She felt his sigh ruffle her hair. "No, I guess we won't."

He held her for a long, long time, until her tears had stopped flowing and her sobs finally subsided.

He held her as she drifted into a restless sleep.

She woke often, sometimes lying drained and tearful from churning emotions, sometimes with her mind racing as she geared up for the fight of her life with Brock the next day.

Every time she awoke, she found Luke holding her tight.

THEY BARELY SPOKE at all on the drive back to Dallas.

During the night, Luke had thought Carly would never stop crying. This morning, every time he glanced across the truck's cab, she sat dry-eyed and staring straight ahead through the windshield.

She must have had her mind focused partly on the conversation she would soon have with Brock.

The rest of her thoughts had to be wrapped up in her guilt from the story she'd told him last night.

Gripping the steering wheel, he turned into the Roughneck's long drive and tried to think of what he would say to her when he dropped her off at the house.

The news about the baby had stunned him. How would he have reacted if she'd told him at the time? He couldn't say. But even at twenty, he knew, he'd have done right by Carly and the child they would have had.

Yet, last night, after he had thought about Carly and the baby, his mind had flown to Rosie. The child he *did* have. The daughter he loved.

Carly couldn't love her, didn't even want a family of her own. He had found a reason for that in the way she had always felt lost in the crowd of her family. He could blame her childhood trauma, laying the guilt at her mom's feet for abandoning them all. But at heart, he couldn't deny he was partly—a damned big part—at fault for the way Carly felt.

He pulled into the parking area outside the ranch house. The front door opened abruptly, as if someone inside had been lying in wait for their return.

At the threshold, Brock sat in his wheelchair.

"Carly—" Luke began.

"I see him." She said the words in a flat tone. For a moment, she stared levelly through the windshield. Then she shoved the door open and climbed from the truck.

He hurried to do the same.

They hadn't gotten within ten yards of the porch when Brock erupted.

"Where the hell have you been with my little girl?" he demanded. "And why the hell haven't you started packing?"

Beside him, Carly stumbled to a halt. She looked

at him, her eyes wide, her face pale. *"Packing?"* she echoed. "Luke?"

"If I had known you were going to stoop to this," Brock said, "I wouldn't have given you a week's notice. I'd have kicked your ass off my ranch the day I fired you."

"*Fired?* Luke? Why didn't you tell me?"

He could see the dismay in her face and the pain in her eyes, just as he had years ago. Then, she had accused him of using her to get what he wanted. Of betraying her for the sake of a job.

Was that what she thought now? That he'd betrayed her again? That he'd slept with her last night to try to save his position at the Roughneck?

Unable to ask those questions in front of his soon-to-be-ex-boss, he simply shrugged.

"What the hell has been going on?" Brock demanded.

"That, Daddy, is exactly what I want to know."

Luke looked from Carly to the older man and back again. The answer to Brock's question was between the pair of them.

Luke nodded his farewell, then turned and walked away.

FOR THE FIRST TIME in her life, Carly closed the door of the den without waiting for the direction from Brock. At this hour of the early afternoon, only Anna would be in the house. She loved and trusted Anna, but this was one conversation she didn't want anyone to overhear.

She held on to to the doorknob, trying to rein in her thoughts. Trying not to envision Luke walking away from her without another word. Again.

Yet, after what she had told him last night, how could she expect anything else?

After a moment, she crossed her arms over her chest and turned to face the room.

Still in his wheelchair, Brock sat behind the desk. His eyes, piercing and blue, met hers calmly, but in the tight skin at their corners and the deep furrows in his brow, she could read his anger clearly.

She hoped he could read hers. "Why did you fire Luke?"

"I don't need a reason—"

"Of course you do. You're a tough boss, but you're fair. You wouldn't let anyone go without cause."

For a moment, she thought he would refuse to answer. Finally, he said, "You're right, there. And I don't keep anyone on my payroll I can't trust. Catching that bastard in the barn with his hands all over you doesn't fit my definition of *trustworthy*."

She couldn't hold back a gasp. "You saw us in the barn?"

"Funny, that was his first question, too. Are you planning to try to lie your way out of it?"

"Did he?" And was an outright lie any worse than just refusing to talk about something? He had kept the news about getting fired from her.

Just as she had kept her secret from him.

"No, he didn't lie," Brock said in a grudging tone.

"You can't fire him for what you saw, Daddy. I was as involved as he was. In fact, I started it."

He said nothing.

"Who did you tell about firing Luke?"

"No one."

"Not even Julieta?"

"I said, no one."

"Good." She moved to stand opposite him and placed her hands flat on the desk. "You need to retract that."

"I'll be damned if I will."

"I'll be damned if you won't."

He reared back, gripping the arms of the chair. "You watch your mouth, little girl."

Despite her anger at him and her concern for Luke, his final words took her temper down a few notches. She shook her head. "He's never given you any reason not to trust him before now, has he?"

He looked back at her without speaking.

"I know he hasn't, or he would have been long gone." She sighed. "You can't blame him when it wasn't his fault. And I know you don't want to hear this, but you can't make him pay for something *I* wanted."

He said nothing, but his grip relaxed.

She waited.

He slapped the arms of the chair. "I've always said you'll be the death of me, Carly."

The tic in his cheek told her he'd swallowed a smile.

She released the breath she'd been holding. She didn't hold back on her smile. "And you're probably going to make me gray before my time. We're two of a kind. Now...Luke's still ranch manager?"

"Yes, dammit."

She leaned across the desk to kiss his cheek. "I'll always be your little girl, Daddy," she said softly. "But you've got to let me live my life. There are times you have to let up on wanting to protect me. This is one of them.

"And now, there's something else we need to get settled." She took a seat in one of the visitors' chairs. She felt grateful it had arms for her to hang on to just as Brock had gripped the wheelchair. "I know you won't want to hear this, either, but I need your help. I want to find Mom."

His shoulders stiffened again. His face lost all expression. "There's not a thing I can do about that."

"I think there is. I need contact info for her."

He shook his head. "I have none."

She stared at him. He held her gaze. He could have any number of reasons for hiding the information, yet she felt certain he had spoken the truth.

She told him about her visit with Mrs. Lewis and what the woman had said about Delia planning to contact him. "I need whatever information you have about her."

"Can't help you there, either."

This time, she sensed he was holding back. "Can't or won't?"

He didn't respond.

"Nothing good comes of keeping secrets, Daddy." Didn't she know that only too well? "Tell me, at least, why she met with you."

As Luke had said, they couldn't prove Delia had even followed through on her intention. And even if she had, Brock could deny ever having seen her.

She held her breath and waited. And waited.

He pushed aside a notepad, centered his pen on top of it, folded his hands on the desk. His movements were controlled, his face calm. Only his white knuckles gave away his tension. "She wanted to get in touch with you kids."

She gasped. "To come home?"

"No. She asked for visitation rights. I denied them— as any judge would once he was informed a woman had abandoned her children and made no attempt to see them in over a year."

"There might have been reasons—"

"Damn her reasons." His voice had grown colder than she had ever heard it. "She had walked out, and Lizzie and Savannah were finally coming to terms with that. You and Jet had no memory of her."

That's not true!

He shook his head. "There was no way in hell I would let her waltz back in and get everyone all riled up again."

She heard the finality in his tone and knew the time had come to quit pushing him. She had gotten all the concessions she could hope for in one day.

Chapter Eighteen

Brock was sitting in the den when his wife arrived home from the office. He had turned the desk lamp on and sat staring at the file folder containing the list of equipment his ranch manager recommended they purchase.

As usual, Luke had done a damned good job. The info was complete, well organized and within budget for the ranch.

He heard Julieta's footsteps, and a moment later she stood in the doorway.

"What are you doing sitting here in the gloom?" she asked.

"Paperwork. It wasn't dark when I started."

She turned on a table lamp and took a seat on the edge of the desk, close to him. She touched his cheek and smiled. "You look broody. What's going on?"

"I've been thinking deep thoughts."

"Such as?"

"The need a man has to protect his family."

"Ah. Even when *they* don't feel the need for that protection?"

"Especially then."

"We're talking about Carly, I presume."

"Danged girl. She said I'm going to make her gray before her time. And that we're two of kind."

Julieta laughed. "She's right. Isn't it just what I've been trying to tell you?"

He rested his hand on her leg. "I've also been thinking about the importance of a man's word. When he lays down the law with another man, he shouldn't go back on that decision."

"I don't know… That would depend on the circumstances when he made it, wouldn't it?"

"How so?"

"His state of mind. The firmness of his conviction. How much knowledge he had of the situation."

He nodded.

He'd gotten firsthand knowledge of Luke's shenanigans in the barn in broad daylight. Still, to hear Carly tell it, she carried the brunt of the responsibility.

She would never sacrifice anyone else for something she'd done. He believed that. On the other hand, there were plenty of days he'd called her and the other kids one by one into this very room, trying to get to the bottom of some mischief. After all the times she'd stood closed-mouthed in front of him, he also trusted she wouldn't have taken on blame she didn't own.

"A man's word might be his bond," Julieta added, "but all those issues have to come into play."

"I see why I hired you to work at Baron Energies."

She laughed. "For the same reasons you married me? Looks and brains—a combination you couldn't pass up."

"Those. And heart." He took her hand. "Especially heart."

He thought about what Luke had said the day he'd fired him.

I love Rosie as much as you love Carly. And I admit, in your shoes, I'd probably do the same.

You had to respect a man who could see both sides of a situation.

When the circumstances warranted.

He thought of the questions Carly had asked about Delia and the answers he'd given her. Sometimes, there was no need to doubt your convictions.

Still, he had to admit he'd been damned proud of his little girl. She had stood up to him over firing the man who had become like another son to him. And she'd given him the knowledge he'd needed to change his mind.

CARLY CALLED LUKE to let him know his job was safe. She owed him that. But before he could ask any questions, she had said goodbye and hung up the phone.

A short while later, at the Peach Pit, she shared with Savannah and Travis the results of her meeting with Mrs. Lewis.

"That's encouraging news, Carly," Travis assured her. "At least it tells us Delia might not have left the state. I'll see what I can find in the Fort Worth area."

She had also told them about her discussion with Brock.

He made a note on the pad in front of him, then looked at her again. "Do you think it's worth pressing your dad for information?"

She shook her head. "Not now. I think I've gotten everything from him he's willing to give."

"There's still hope Mrs. Lewis can find an address," Savannah said.

"Yes," Carly agreed, trying to sound optimistic. Trying to sound as though she had any enthusiasm at all. The new information the trip to Lubbock had provided only strengthened her determination to find her mom.

But what had happened with Luke on their arrival home had broken her heart.

Considering all the touchy subjects they had covered in just the past few days, she would have thought he could tell her the truth about being fired. But, obviously, he still hadn't trusted her enough.

After what she had told him the night before, she couldn't blame him if he never trusted her again.

Desperate to keep herself from thinking of him, she stayed at the store until closing time.

Afterward, she didn't go directly home. Halfway there, even as she coasted up the long drive to the ranch house, she finally acknowledged to herself the decision she had made the minute she had said goodbye to Luke.

She had to talk to him. But not over the phone.

His job was safe now. He would stay here as manager.

As for what she would do...

She had just begun to let herself dream of returning to the Roughneck permanently. Of going into partnership with Savannah at the store. But the thought of living on the ranch and having to face Luke and Rosie was almost more than she could bear.

She had slept with Luke, opened her heart to him, confessed the secret she'd kept from him all these years. He had held her last night—held her *all* night. She hadn't wanted that to end. She didn't want her reunion with Luke to be over, either. And yet, this afternoon, he had rejected her, refusing to answer her questions and walking away.

No matter how hard it would be to face him now, she had to. They could never have a relationship. She would have to leave. But she didn't want to let everything end the way it had the first time.

She had to find out why he hadn't told her Brock had

fired him and whether he had planned to leave the ranch without telling her. To walk away without a word, just as he had that afternoon and as he'd done years ago.

Outside his house, there was no sign of Tammy's small car. Luke's truck sat in its usual space near the back porch.

When he answered her knock at the door, he looked stunned to see her.

"Can I come in?"

He stepped back from the doorway.

In the living room, he took the chair and leaned forward, resting his forearms on his thighs and linking his fingers together.

She wanted to curl up on his couch with her knees close to her and her arms wrapped around them. A defensive pose, she realized now. Just another way to hide.

She took a seat on the couch and stretched her booted feet out in front of her. "This afternoon, you wouldn't answer me. After…after last night, I had hoped we could tell each other anything." She took a deep breath and continued, "What's going on? Why wouldn't you tell me about getting fired?"

To her surprise, he gave her a half smile and shook his head. "'What's going on?'" he repeated. "That's what Brock said. You really are Daddy's little cowgirl, aren't you?"

"Yes. And I always will be."

"Not a surprise. You always were." He was thinking of the past.

"This afternoon, why did you walk away without answering me?"

He hesitated.

Her heart sank. "It's because I never told you about the baby, isn't it?"

"You were almost a kid back then yourself. How could I blame you for not telling me?"

"You could be unfair about it," she said honestly, her voice breaking. "Just as unfair as I was to you."

"Two wrongs?" He shook his head. "Some folks might go for that, but you already know I don't work that way."

He rose and went to stand by one of the curio cabinets. She could see his reflection in the mirrored wall inside. He had something he didn't want to tell her. But whatever it was, she needed to hear it.

"No more secrets, Luke." When he remained quiet, she continued, "I didn't talk much on the ride home this morning, partly because I was thinking about having to talk to my daddy. I could feel you backing off, too." She swallowed hard. "I apologize again for not telling you everything until last night. I'm sorry about the baby. So very sorry. If I could change that…if I could change anything that happened…I would."

"You can't take all the blame on yourself. I'm just as much at fault. If I had given you my reason for wanting the job with your daddy, I could have saved you all that hurt you went through."

"Luke—"

He turned to face her. "It's true. If I'd told you, we might still be together now. And…"

"And we might still have our child." She had to blink to see him clearly through her tears. He looked as miserable as she felt. "I'm more guilty than you are for jumping to conclusions and not giving you a chance to explain."

He shrugged again. "When it comes right down to it, guilt doesn't matter. Neither does the past."

"What does, then?"

"The future." He sighed. "I can forget the idea of giving Rosie a brother or sister or two. But there's more. I backed off from you because there's no way I can have a relationship with someone who can't accept Rosie in her life."

"Oh, Luke." Her laugh sounded more like a sob. "I know I told you marriage and family weren't in my plans. That was only because I didn't think I deserved them. Not after losing our baby. But another reason I didn't talk on the ride back is because I was starting to panic."

"Panic?"

"At the thought of leaving here again. Leaving you and Rosie. She won my heart this week," she said softly. "And you won it a long time ago. If you don't already know that."

He smiled.

"You were right," she admitted. "To find out where I truly belong, I had to figure out where I'm happiest. Now I have." She laughed. "We already know it's not on the back of a bull. And it's not in Houston, either."

"I've always known that."

She smiled. "I can't hide behind a mask now. And I can't act like a wild child with you. I can only be myself and tell you what I really feel. I love you."

"I've always known that, too."

"Luke!"

"I'll tell you one more thing I've always known." He crossed the room and pulled her to her feet. Then he took her into his arms. "I love you, too. And no matter what happened between the day we met and now, I've always known you belong with me."

"With you and Rosie," she corrected. "And with all our future little cowgirls and cowboys."

Epilogue

Two weeks later

Carly looked down at the jeweler's bag in her lap. "This is going to seem a little crazy to my family— Us, coming home with a couple of wedding rings and plans to get married at Christmastime, when we haven't told them we've gotten engaged. Because we haven't *officially* gotten engaged yet."

Luke parked the truck, then reached across the cab and squeezed her hand. "Hey, aren't you the girl who always does what folks *don't* expect?"

"Not anymore."

He laughed.

Frowning, she looked through the windshield. "Jacob's truck is here. So is Lizzie's car. Something's up."

He followed her into the ranch house. A burst of laughter from the direction of the dining room made her hurry in that direction. All the Barons were gathered around the table, in the middle of which sat a huge cake.

"What's this?" she demanded. "A family celebration, and I wasn't invited?"

"Oh, you're invited, all right," Jet assured her. "We'd never leave you out." He gestured to the empty chair beside him.

"We couldn't even celebrate the good news without you here," Jacob said.

"More good news?" She had already told her family she was moving back home again. And she and Savannah had announced their plan to become partners.

She looked at Brock, seated at the head of the table.

He smiled but shook his head. "Not from me."

She looked around the table at the faces of her family. Anna was there, too, seated between Lizzie and Alex. Everyone looked excited, as if they had already heard the news. "All right, then. What's going on?"

Luke put his hand on her shoulder, just as he had that night at the Longhorn. And just like that night, his touch set off a heat low inside her. She turned in her chair to look at him.

He was down on one knee, smiling up at her. "I thought we would make this official now, in front of your family."

She smiled. "I can't think of anything I'd like better."

He pulled a ring from his pocket. "Carly Baron, will you marry me and be Rosie's mom?"

She blinked away the tears that sprang to her eyes. She had waited so long for this. "Yes. And yes."

After he slipped the ring onto her finger, she leaned forward to kiss him.

Everyone in the room cheered.

Daniel opened a bottle of champagne and Anna began slicing cake.

Jet offered the toast. "A big thank-you to Luke for helping us exceed quota."

"What does that mean?" Luke asked her.

Carly was laughing so hard, she almost spilled her champagne. Once she could speak again, she said, "I'll explain later."

When the party was over and they were driving home, she said, "Did you see how happy Daddy looked at getting you for a son-in-law?"

"He is happy. At least, that's what he told me when I went to ask his permission to marry you."

"You asked his *permission?* And what did he say?"

"He thanked me for taking his little girl off his hands."

She laughed. "I'll bet he did." As they went up the porch steps, she added, "Speaking of little girls, what time is Rosie coming home?"

"She's not. Mom's keeping her overnight." He ushered her into the house. "I thought we might want to continue the celebration."

"I think you're right." She closed the door firmly behind them.

He tilted her chin up and kissed her. "I'm glad you came back," he murmured.

"I am, too," she said. She thought of her family, who all loved her. Of Rosie, who snuggled against her every morning when she picked her up from her crib. Of Luke, who had always known her better than she had known herself.

She thought of how busy and chaotic and full of family her life would be from that point forward. And she smiled. "Coming home," she assured him, "was the best decision I've ever made."

* * * * *

Follow the continuing saga of the
TEXAS RODEO BARONS *in Pamela Britton's book*
THE TEXAN'S TWINS,
available from Harlequin American Romance
in September 2014!

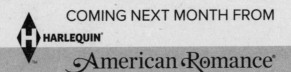

REQUEST YOUR FREE BOOKS!
2 FREE NOVELS PLUS 2 *FREE GIFTS!*

⊕ HARLEQUIN®

American ★ Romance®

LOVE, HOME & HAPPINESS

YES! Please send me 2 FREE Harlequin® American Romance® novels and my 2 FREE gifts (gifts are worth about $10). After receiving them, if I don't wish to receive any more books, I can return the shipping statement marked "cancel." If I don't cancel, I will receive 4 brand-new novels every month and be billed just $4.74 per book in the U.S. or $5.24 per book in Canada. That's a savings of at least 14% off the cover price! It's quite a bargain! Shipping and handling is just 50¢ per book in the U.S. and 75¢ per book in Canada.* I understand that accepting the 2 free books and gifts places me under no obligation to buy anything. I can always return a shipment and cancel at any time. Even if I never buy another book, the two free books and gifts are mine to keep forever.

154/354 HDN F4YN

Name _____ (PLEASE PRINT) _____

Address _____ Apt. #

City _____ State/Prov. _____ Zip/Postal Code

Signature (if under 18, a parent or guardian must sign)

Mail to the **Harlequin®** Reader Service:
IN U.S.A.: P.O. Box 1867, Buffalo, NY 14240-1867
IN CANADA: P.O. Box 609, Fort Erie, Ontario L2A 5X3

**Want to try two free books from another line?
Call 1-800-873-8635 or visit www.ReaderService.com.**

* Terms and prices subject to change without notice. Prices do not include applicable taxes. Sales tax applicable in N.Y. Canadian residents will be charged applicable taxes. Offer not valid in Quebec. This offer is limited to one order per household. Not valid for current subscribers to Harlequin American Romance books. All orders subject to credit approval. Credit or debit balances in a customer's account(s) may be offset by any other outstanding balance owed by or to the customer. Please allow 4 to 6 weeks for delivery. Offer available while quantities last.

Your Privacy—The Harlequin® Reader Service is committed to protecting your privacy. Our Privacy Policy is available online at www.ReaderService.com or upon request from the Harlequin Reader Service.

We make a portion of our mailing list available to reputable third parties that offer products we believe may interest you. If you prefer that we not exchange your name with third parties, or if you wish to clarify or modify your communication preferences, please visit us at www.ReaderService.com/consumerschoice or write to us at Harlequin Reader Service Preference Service, P.O. Box 9062, Buffalo, NY 14269. Include your complete name and address.

HAR13R

"You going to take off your dress now? Or later?"

The woman's eyes widened. *"Excuse me?"*

"Don't worry. My friends didn't know I was meeting a man. A project engineer, actually, and you don't exactly look the part. Nice try, though."

"Let me guess—Jet Baron."

"One and the same." He gave her a welcoming smile, his gaze slowly sliding over her body.

"Why am I *not* surprised?" she asked.

Her sarcasm startled him, as did the way she eyed him up and down. So direct. So appraising. So…disappointed.

He straightened. "If you're going to start stripping, you better do it now. I'm expecting the engineer at any moment."

"You think I'm some kind of prank. An actress hired to, what? Pretend to have a meeting with you? Then strip out of my clothes?"

He was starting to get a funny feeling. "Well, yeah."

She took a step toward him, and he would be lying if he didn't feel as if, somehow, the joke was on him.

"Tell me something, what makes you think the engineer in question is a man?"

"I was told that."

"By whom?"

"I don't know who told me, I just know he's a man. All engineers in the oil industry are men."

She took another step toward him. "There are actually quite a few women in the business. I graduated from Berkley with a degree in geology." She took yet another step closer. "I interned for the USGS out of Menlo Park then moved back to Texas to get my master's in engineering. My father was a wildcatter, and it was from him that I learned the business—so let me reassure you, Mr. Baron, I can tell the difference between an injection hose and a drill pipe. But if you still insist only men can be engineers, perhaps we should call your sister, Lizzie, who hired me."

Jet couldn't speak for a moment. "Oh, crap."

Her extraordinary blue eyes scanned him, her derision clearly evident. "Still want me to strip?"

He almost said yes, but he could tell that he was in enough trouble as it is. "I take it you're J.C.?"

"I am."

"I should apologize."

"You think?"

Look for THE TEXAN'S TWINS
by Pamela Britton next month from
Harlequin® American Romance®.

American Romance®

Triple the Trouble

When fertility counselor Melissa Everhart decided to have a baby on her own, she didn't anticipate triplets…or her ex-husband's return to Safe Harbor. Three years ago, Edmond's reluctance to have children tore them apart. But now that he's been made guardian of his niece, Melissa witnesses how tenderly he cares for the little girl.

Though Edmond doesn't believe he's father material, his sudden custody of Dawn leaves him little choice. He turns to Melissa, the warmest, kindest person he knows, for help. They begin to rediscover the love they once shared, but the betrayals of the past trouble them both. Can they find the forgiveness they both need to come together as a family?

Look for
The Surprise Triplets
by JACQUELINE DIAMOND

from the *Safe Harbor Medical* miniseries from
Harlequin® American Romance®.

Available September 2014
wherever books and ebooks are sold.

Also available from the *Safe Harbor Medical* miniseries
by Jacqueline Diamond:
A Baby for the Doctor
The Surprise Holiday Dad
His Baby Dream
The Baby Jackpot

American Romance®

A Little Bit Country…

Emma Donovan ran off to Nashville when she was
young and full of dreams. Now she's back home in
Colorado with a little more common sense.
And that sense is telling her not to count on
Jamie Westland. He won't be around long—not
with his big-time career in New York City.

Jamie's never felt at home, not with his adopted family,
not with himself. Now, on his grandfather's ranch,
the pieces of his life are coming together in a way that
feels right. And Emma has so much to do with it.
But when an opportunity comes along back in New York,
he has to decide between his old life and the promise
of a new one…with Emma.

Cowboy in the Making
by JULIE BENSON

Available September 2014
wherever books and ebooks are sold.